ALWAYS YOU

A BEST FRIENDS TO LOVERS ROMANCE

MEGAN HART

Always You

Megan Hart

Chaos Publishing

———

BLURB

Jack and Josie have a game.

Ten points for correctly predicting which lame come-on the next person will use to hit on you. Fifteen points for getting asked for your phone number. Twenty for being bought a drink.

Get someone to ask you to go home with them, and you've won The Game.

Now Josie's tired of watching beautiful women throw themselves at the one man who's always been there for her, and even winning has become losing if it means the man who takes her home from the bar isn't Jack. She knows how to get other men to fall at her feet, but will the same moves work on her best friend? In love and lust, it's all about Playing The Game...

Jack and Josie have been friends for years, but what will it take to convince them it's time to become more?

Always You includes Playing the Game, Opening the Door and White Wedding, three novellas from the author of best-selling novels Dirty, Broken, Tempted and more.

PLAYING THE GAME

ONE

Josie took the bottle of beer from the cute bartender, being sure to make eye contact. "Thanks."

"No problem. Any time." He smiled and gave her a nod.

She read the gleam of interest in his eyes. She could have continued the flirtation, but her heart just wasn't in it. She gave him another smile anyway because he really was cute and shoved her lime down to the bottom of the bottle. She took a swig, relishing the tang of the cool liquid on the back of her throat. It was her third beer tonight, when her normal limit was two. She was feeling bored, and a little reckless.

The bar was getting crowded. The thump of dance music reverberated in her belly. She scanned the row of low benches against the railing that separated the bar area from the dance floor. Her heart jumped, as it always did lately, when she saw the tall, broad-shouldered man clad in the tight, gray t-shirt and jeans. She finished her beer in four gulps, and to her own surprise, called for another.

The man sitting at one of the high top booths almost directly across from her on the other side of the dance floor had a wide mouth with full lips that looked like they could drive a woman to her knees with one kiss. Dark, laughing eyes. Smooth, perfectly shaped ears boasted a gold hoop in each lobe. He'd shaved his dark hair close to his scalp, and though it wasn't a look she normally liked, on him it worked.

He saw her looking, and his lips curved into a slow, sexy smile that made her shift against the bar and take another drink. He waggled his eyebrows at her and blew her a kiss. Josie couldn't help it. She laughed. Shaking her head, she left the bar and crossed to the bench.

"Jack, you're insane."

Jack took Josie's hand and pulled her down to his lap as she tried to edge by him. His breath whispered on her ear as he said, "Which one did you pick out for yourself tonight?"

Josie ducked her head away from his tickling mouth and elbowed him until he let her slide from his lap to the seat beside him. "None. But I'm sure you have half a dozen picked out already."

His low, deep chuckle was loud enough to turn the head of the pretty blonde standing across from them at the bar. Her eyes took in Jack from head to toe, and the woman practically licked her lips. Jack slid his arm across Josie's shoulder and lifted his chin toward the blonde, who returned the gesture with a smirk of her own. Her gaze flickered over Josie, apparently dismissing her as no threat, and then she earned ten points for Jack with her next move.

"There it is," Jack murmured. He bent close to Josie's ear again. His voice was so deep it sounded like thunder, even when he whispered. "The hair toss. I get ten points."

Josie had to lift the bottle to her mouth to hide the grin. "I'll bet you those ten her next move is the buckle adjustment."

"I'll take that bet." Jack's fingers ran slowly along Josie's arm, along the back of her neck and rested there. "I think she's going for the olive suck."

Josie and Jack had been coming to The Pharmacy for years to play The Game. The rules were simple. They each got points for predicting which tactics members of the opposite sex would use to flirt with them. Additional points were gained by being given phone numbers, being asked to dance, being bought a drink, being asked to go home—all without either of them using any of the common flirting moves. They'd started The Game because Josie had become so adept at being able to tell how far women would go to gain Jack's attention. Jack, who since childhood had never allowed Josie to best him in anything, had taken up the challenge.

They usually arrived together, but they didn't always leave together. There'd been many times Jack had won The Game simply by default—he'd chosen to take some hottie's offer of breakfast in the morning, while Josie had preferred to head home by herself, wash the smoke out of her hair and slip into her quiet bed, alone.

The Game had seen them through high school, college, heartaches, and lost jobs. Tonight was the first time they'd played in about a year—since before Josie began dating Barry. The relationship had soured, as they always seemed to do, and had put a bad taste in her mouth toward men. Jack had insisted playing The Game would cheer her up. She wasn't convinced.

Now Jack's thigh pressed intimately against Josie's. His hand still cupped her neck. They watched together as the blonde at the bar set down her drink, then, with a discreet glance to make certain she still had Jack's attention, she bent to toy with the buckle of her stiletto heeled shoe. The move caused her mini-skirt to ride even further up her tanned thigh, exposing just the hint of lacy underwear. She straightened, apparently satisfied with her shoe, and turned her back on Jack and Josie.

Jack threw back his head and groaned. Josie poked his chest. "That's your cue to go up to her. And that's my ten points."

As Josie spoke, the blonde turned, drink in hand, and lifted the toothpick-speared olive from her martini to her perfectly glossed lips. She closed her mouth around the olive and pulled it slowly off the pick in a gesture so seductive it was almost a parody of itself.

"There!" Jack said.

"Too late," Josie countered. "She did the shoe thing first. Go get her."

Jack leaned back and put his arm over Josie's shoulder again. His fingers stroked the wispy hairs at the back of her neck. He shrugged. "Nah."

After a few minutes, the blonde gave Jack another sultry look, which he didn't catch because he was too busy checking out the dance floor. Josie watched the blonde frown, then glance over her again. The woman's gaze took in Jack's casually draped hand, and the way it toyed now and then with one of Josie's dangling earrings. She arched her eyebrows and said something to her companion, an equally predatory looking brunette. Both women turned to stare at Josie, who by now had shivers running up and down her spine from Jack's hand playing with her earring.

"Stop it." She slapped at his hand. "You're driving me nuts."

He stopped touching the dangling silver chain at her ear and moved his arm. The blonde and her friend had moved off toward the dance floor. "Hey, we lost her."

"*You* lost her." Josie inched over on the crowded bench,

ignoring the way the guy next to her seemed to take it as an excuse to fix a beer-bleary smile on her. "You took too long. She lost interest."

Jack looked behind her to the dance floor again. One of his large hands splayed unconsciously against the chest of his tight gray t-shirt. His fingers tapped in time to the beat.

"Yeah, I guess," he said absent-mindedly. "Hey, Josie, let's go dance."

"Yeah?" she asked, surprised. "You're tired of The Game already?"

Jack's grin was hot enough to melt butter. He leaned forward so close she smelled the mint of his gum mixed with the spicy, musky scent of his cologne. "Why? You got somebody picked out?"

His smell had suddenly become more intoxicating than the beer she'd been sipping. Josie swallowed against a dry throat. She pulled away, again bumping the man beside her.

"Not really," she said.

Jack gave her a puzzled look. "You all right?"

She wasn't all right, but Josie didn't tell him that. "Fine. Let's dance."

"Let me hit the john, and I'll be right back."

He tugged a strand of her hair, then headed off through the crowd. Josie watched him go, the view from behind as delightful as that from the front. His dark pants clung just right to his tight ass, and the gray t-shirt fit him like a second skin across his muscled shoulders and back. Jack dodged the crowd with a liquid grace that melted her insides.

Stop it! She tossed back the last few swigs of beer and got up to set it on the table. She refused the guy next to her's offer of another and ran her hands over her hair to smooth it from the tangling Jack had given it.

He's just a friend. Your best friend. You used to bet each other you'd eat worms, for God's sake!

With a shudder, Josie gripped the table's edge. Something was wrong with her tonight, and she couldn't blame it on the extra beer she'd consumed. She'd been feeling this way for the past few months... Hell, since she was being honest with herself, the past few years.

The thudding of her heart seemed to move in time with the throbbing dance music. The colored lights on the dance floor flickered in her vision, and Josie had to close her eyes for a minute, disoriented.

She felt him behind her before he said anything. She'd always been in tune with Jack, ever since they were kids playing hide and seek. Lately, though, her body was reacting to Jack's presence a lot differently. Her nipples tightened, her belly dropped. She found herself imagining what it would be like to see him naked—and she'd seen him naked many times without bothering to notice it. Now she wished she'd paid closer attention.

"Ready?"

She turned. "Yep. Let's tear it up!"

He took her hand to lead her to the dance floor. Jack was a big guy, standing just over six feet tall and solid with muscle. He made an easy path for them through the throng to the crowded dance floor.

Dancing was a sure-fire way to get the attention which would gain them points in The Game, but that wasn't the only reason Jack and Josie danced together. Jack really loved to dance and he was very good at it. Despite his tough-guy appearance, Jack could cut a rug to rival Fred Astaire courtesy of a few years of dance lessons their mothers had insisted on. Jack and Josie had little opportunity to foxtrot at places like this, but Jack was as skilled in all styles of dancing as he was at everything else.

Josie loved to dance with Jack. It was comfortable and safe, but also a hell of a good time. She didn't have to worry that a little pelvic thrust would end up with her being tongue-kissed by some idiot with a booze-soaked brain and breath that could knock over an elephant. Josie could dance with Jack and be uninhibited—and she'd had more offers for dates based on what men had seen her do with Jack on the dance floor than anything else. She felt guilty about that, sometimes, like it was false advertising. Then again, it was all just part of The Game.

Jack was already bobbing his close-shaved head. He grinned, his teeth glowing supernaturally white in the dance floor's weird lighting. He made a space for them on the floor by nudging people out of the way.

They bounced to the rhythm for a while. Josie had to return Jack's grin. The last beer she'd had was making her feel giddier than she normally did, and besides that, she was having fun for the first night in the three months since she'd caught Barry in bed with the girl who worked in the dry cleaner's. Hell, she was having more fun than she'd had the entire time she dated Barry.

One song blended seamlessly into the next and became a popular new club hit featuring a sexy salsa beat inter-spersed with the lyrics to a rap song.

"Let's rip it up."

Jack's voice rumbled in her ear and vibrated in her stomach. His grin made her want to grab him and kiss him, but that was just ridiculous—wasn't it? She wasn't here tonight to make out with Jack.

Josie stepped into Jack's arms with the familiarity she never seemed to find with any other man. One hand went to his shoulder; the other disappeared into his much larger palm. Jack's other hand pressed low down on her back, just below the edge of her soft cotton shirt. Oh, mercy. Against her bare skin.

Josie took a deep, shuddering breath, then forced herself to meet Jack's eyes. She couldn't let him know how his touch affected her. He wouldn't understand. *She* didn't understand. When had she stopped thinking of him as a buddy and started wanting him as a lover?

Jack led her effortlessly into a fast, modified cha-cha. Josie was a decent dancer, but under Jack's lead she moved like a dream. The crowd didn't allow them much movement, so while the dance normally kept partners several inches apart, she and Jack moved like they were one person. Her thighs were snugged against his, and her belly pressed into his groin.

Slowly, the people around them seemed to notice something hot was going on and they moved apart to allow Jack and Josie more room to move. The song turned out to be some sort of extended-edit remix and it seemed to go on forever. Jack stopped smiling. His eyes bore into Josie's. The fingers against her back traced light circles on her bare skin, even as he guided her into an increasingly sensuous series of steps.

Josie hadn't dressed for seduction tonight. Short dresses and high heels weren't part of The Game; the goal was to encourage interest without overt measures. Tonight she wore boot-cut jeans, tight on her ass to show off the curve of her hips. Now, with every movement, the snug denim rubbed between her legs in a way that made her want to clench her fists or moan.

She took another deep breath and stared at Jack, who wore a look of deep concentration. Faster they danced, keeping up with the beat, making up their own moves. He pulled her close enough so her breasts, unfettered beneath her white cotton baby doll t-shirt, rubbed against his muscled chest. His thigh moved between hers, leading her into moves straight out of Dirty Dancing.

He was playing, but with whom? The blonde from the bar? Some other woman who would gladly trade places with Josie on the dance floor? Jack was really putting his all into the dance, and for the first time, Josie felt out of control in Jack's arms.

She was helpless against the sensations rocketing through her as he slid his hand from her back to the curve of her ass. His hand was large enough to cover most of her rear. After a minute, he let go of her hand to put his other hand on her rear, too.

The song changed, and the crowd, no longer impressed with fancy footwork, moved in again. Over Jack's shoulder, Josie saw the blonde from the bar. Envy was clearly stamped on her pretty face, and her eyes were riveted to the way Jack's ass moved to the beat of a new song.

Josie was used to seeing looks of such hunger when women, and sometimes men, looked at Jack. This time, though, the sight didn't make her want to laugh. She wanted to slap the bitch's face, or she wanted to cry, because she knew how the other woman felt.

Josie closed her eyes as Jack pulled her even closer. She touched her forehead to his shoulder briefly. He wasn't doing anything he hadn't done a hundred times before. In fact, some nights when The Game was in full swing, he'd done far racier things with her to gain the attention of some hapless victim.

Those other nights, Josie hadn't minded. It had all been a part of The Game. Tonight was different. Tonight, when he pulled her close and nuzzled her neck, she had to fight not to check and see if his eyes were closed or looking over her shoulder to attract someone else. And was that the nip of his teeth on her skin? The slick wetness of the tip of his tongue?

Josie's nipples stretched the fabric of her thin shirt. Jack's mouth pressed the spot where her pulse pounded fast, and not only from exertion.

She stepped out of Jack's arms and turned her back to him. Lots of other couples and even trios were doing the same move; the move had become very popular in the clubs. Jack, without missing a beat, put his hands on her hips and snugged her ass tight against his crotch. Her every nerve pulled taut at the sensation of his hard body against hers.

Josie cursed herself as she let Jack rock her back against him. She searched the crowd in front of them. Who was he hard for? The blonde, or the sexy, older woman with upswept gray hair that reflected purple under the strobe lights? It can't be the redhead, even though her tits were the size of melons. Jack had always joked with Josie that redheads didn't turn him on.

His hands slid from her hips to her waist. The song became another, impossibly faster. The crowd moved as one entity, crushing, grinding and rocking with the rhythm. She had no room to move away from Jack; no room to breathe.

She'd drunk too much. That had to be the explanation. One beer too many, and she was horny as hell, too. That might have something to do with it. She hadn't slept with anyone in three months. Drunk and horny and dancing with Jack—not a good combination, but as the crowd dipped and bounced around them, Josie couldn't bring herself to leave.

She arched her back, just a little, to rest the back of her

head on Jack's chest. His lips found her temple, and the ridge of her cheek. Josie slid her hands down the bulge of his forearms to place them over Jack's hands on her waist. The dark, crisp hair tickled her fingertips, and she shivered. Her mouth parted, like she was trying to gasp, but there was no air to take in.

Drowning. She was drowning in a sea of sexual tension. It rolled across the dance floor and hovered in the air thicker than the haze of cigarette smoke. It smelled like the tang of sweat, the musk of cologne, the sweet bite of alcohol.

Her clit rubbed mercilessly against the silk of her panties. Slickness coated her. She rocked her hips upward, and the tug of her denim jeans against her aroused flesh sent shocks of pleasure rippling through her.

Josie could, if the mood was right, get herself off merely by squeezing her thighs together. The mood was definitely right, even if she didn't want it to be. This was no active choice; no furtive movement at her desk designed to relieve the boredom of a long afternoon at work. She had no control over this. Everything was the music, the beer, Jack's hands on her and his breath on her face.

Josie arched against him again, ashamed of the intensity of her arousal, and afraid of what he'd do if he knew. The temptation of climax was too powerful a motivation to deny, especially since she hadn't had an orgasm in so long. Sex with Barry had been lackluster, and finally nonexistent, but she'd been so depressed after yet another failed relationship that she hadn't even touched herself since they'd broken up.

Her body needed release, and craved it. If she kept dancing with Jack, Josie had no doubt she would achieve it. Guilt forced her to move away from him as much as she could with the crowd as dense as it was. She would be using him, and he wouldn't even know it. He was too good of a friend for her to do that.

Just as she decided to step away from him altogether and go to the bathroom for a cold splash of water, another new song came on. Not only did it have a driving rhythm, the lyrics were suggestive and sexy. The song had become an anthem of sorts for the singles looking for lust in Harrisburg's hot spots.

"Down on your knees, baby please." The men in the crowd shouted the words to the women they pursued. The women answered along with the female vocalist. "Let your tongue give me, give me what I need."

The song's popularity sent people who hadn't been dancing onto the floor. The crowd swelled and surged. Josie was tossed with it, her ass pressed even further against Jack's crotch. He curved his fingers on her waist to protect her from the crush. He pulled her with him, back toward the wall where there was a little more space. Two steps, three, and Jack hit the black-painted boards, Josie's back still snug against his chest.

Instantly, people filled the space they'd left behind. The song pounded on, words of lust and love, degradation and devotion, a paean to sex and sin.

"Down on your knees!"

Josie's hands clenched on top of Jack's.

"Give me what I need!"

The crowd roared.

"Slide it in me, baby, please!"

Josie reached up and behind her to touch Jack's neck and the back of his smoothly shaved head as she arched her back again. He took his hands from her waist, slid them up her sides and cupped her breasts.

"I wanna fuck you, baby! Wanna make you come!"

Each hand covered her completely. His palms caressed her nipples. Josie tried to breathe and couldn't, then had to close her eyes when the flashing lights made her head spin.

She caressed the line of his jaw and drew his mouth back to her temple. He kissed her, his lips hot on her skin. The floor vibrated with the stomps of a hundred pairs of feet moving at the same time. Josie stood on her toes to push herself back further, to let Jack's mouth find the corner of her own.

The song was reaching its climax, and oh mercy, so was she. Josie fought it, hated herself for it, but it felt so good, too damn good. She couldn't fight it, couldn't resist. She was on the edge, nearly there...

Oh, please...

As the song reached its final throbbing notes, Jack put one hand between her legs. His hand cupped her groin; the heel of his palm pressed just where she needed it most. Separated from his touch by a layer of denim and silk, nonetheless Josie was so close she needed only the slightest pressure to explode.

She splintered into a myriad of shining pieces. The world closed down until all she saw was the blue, the red, the flashing purple and green. All she felt was Jack against her. She smelled him, and dear God, tasted him as his mouth found hers again and he slipped his tongue inside her open lips. She was flying.

With the aftershocks still rippling through her, Josie slammed back into herself. The music had changed to something less popular, and many people had forsaken the dance floor for the solace of the bar. She had space to move again.

She didn't imagine the hungry looks on them. It had been quite a performance. She stepped out of Jack's arms so quickly his hand tugged for a moment between her legs and sent another slow ripple of pleasure through her.

Heat seared her cheeks. Did he know? How could he not? Josie pressed her fingers to her mouth lightly as she started to push her way through the crowd. She'd kissed Jack lots of time before, but never like that. Never really kissed him as a lover would, not even when they were playing The Game.

Guilt assailed her again, even as her body still rocked from the orgasm. She didn't speak as she moved through the crowd, but she sensed him following her.

"Water," she said to the bartender, who nodded solemnly. Had he seen them? Josie looked around. People spoke to each other, their eyes trained on her. She must really have made a spectacle of herself.

She tossed back a gulp of ice water. Jack ordered a Corona. He nudged his way next to her at the bar and took a long swig of his beer.

"Wow." Even speaking only one word, his deep voice rumbled.

Josie couldn't meet his eyes, afraid of what she might see. "I have to go."

Jack put his beer on the bar. "What? Why? Josie, it's still early..."

"I don't feel like playing The Game anymore tonight," she snapped. She sounded angry, and she was angry, but not at him.

She pushed away from the bar and headed for the door. Jack followed a step behind. In the hallway, much emptier than the bar itself, he grabbed her arm hard enough to turn her around.

"What's going on?" he demanded.

Josie forced herself to look at him. Her mouth felt

stretched, frowning, and she bit at her lip. "Nothing. I'm tired. I want to go home."

Jack's sexy grin and cocky laugh made her stomach drop. "I'll come with you."

She put her hand on his chest to stop him from moving toward her. Beneath the gray cotton, she felt the rapid pulse of his heart. Her fingers touched the sharp point of his nipple before she pulled away like she'd been burned.

"No, Jack!" She'd yelled without realizing it.

He stepped back, clearly surprised. "C'mon, Josie, what the hell?"

"Go back inside. Go find some hottie bimbo to take home. You win The Game tonight. I'm done."

He reached for her again, but she danced away from his grasp. "I can't play The Game if you're not here."

For an endless moment, his eyes locked on hers. The hall was lit with a black light that turned Jack's dark eyes into glimmering, shimmering pools. He wasn't grinning any more.

She couldn't speak. For the first time in all their years of friendship, Josie couldn't find the words to tell him how she felt. For the first time, she lied to him. "Leave me alone, damn it! I don't want you to come home with me!"

Without waiting for him to reply, she stalked down the hall and out the door to the street. A light rain had started, and it felt good. Cool on her hot face. It soaked her thin t-shirt, and she crossed her arms around herself, expecting a chill, but the night was warm and the rain gentle.

The door opened behind her and Jack came out. The beat of club music filled the space between them for a second until the door swung closed again. A man and woman, clearly drunk by their laughter and stagger, passed her on their way down the street.

"Josie!"

She started walking. She lived only a few blocks away. Her boots hit the pavement and splashed in the puddles.

"Damn it, Josie, wait up!"

She walked faster.

"Don't walk home by yourself!"

Even now, he was looking out for her. Self-loathing filled her. She'd used him for her own selfish desires, and now her shame wouldn't let her admit it to him.

"I'll be fine," she shot over her shoulder.

There was no getting away from him, of course. He could take one stride for every two of hers and catch up to her in a minute. He grabbed her arm again to stop her.

The glow of the streetlamp highlighted his features. The rain had smoothed the fabric of his t-shirt over the curves of his muscular chest. Water dripped from his eyebrows and chin, and he licked away some drops.

"What's wrong?" he asked. "Josie, what did I do?"

"Nothing, Jack." Josie yanked her arm from his grasp. "Forget it."

"I won't forget it! One minute you're all over me, and the next you're running away!"

Josie slapped her wet hair from her eyes. "Me, all over you? You were the one putting your hands on me!"

He raised an eyebrow at her. "You didn't tell me no."

Anger reared up in her as a way to combat her guilt. "Did I have to? I'm not one of your conquests, Jack! I'm not some bar floozy impressed with the size of your muscles or your cock!"

He actually flinched, as though she'd struck him. "No, Josie. You're not."

Silence hung between them, and again she felt like she couldn't breathe. There was more to be said, but Josie was afraid to say it. Even more afraid to hear it. Jack was the best friend she had. Conversations like this ruined friendships, and she refused to lose him. Not like this.

"I'm going home," she said.

This time, when she turned and walked away he didn't follow her.

"What happened on the dance floor, Josie?" he hollered after her, but she didn't answer.

TWO

By the time she got home, Josie was shivering with delayed reaction. The fourth beer she wanted to blame for her mistakes churned in her gut. A headache had begun to throb in her temples. Worst of all, tears stung her eyes and, as hard as she tried to fight them, they fell to burn her cheeks.

She stripped off her sodden jeans and tossed them over a chair. Her skin hunched into gooseflesh in her apartment's air conditioning, and she turned the thermostat up. The hot shower beckoned her, but she couldn't even take comfort in its spray. She stepped out after the briefest of soapings and dried herself. Naked, she padded to the kitchen and pulled out the first shirt she found in the basket of clean laundry on her kitchen table, and slipped it over her head. When the hem hit her just above the knees, she clutched the soft fabric with a slight moan. The shirt was one of Jack's.

"Shit," Josie swore under her breath.

She heard a knock at the front door and her heart thudded in surprise. She hadn't locked it. Just as she moved into the narrow front hall, the door banged open hard enough to hit the wall.

Jack, dripping, strode into the hall and kicked the door shut behind him. He nearly filled the hall from side to side. Water puddled on the hardwood floor beneath his boots.

Josie stepped back, breathless, and hit the wall behind her. She couldn't move. In seconds, Jack crossed the space between them and put his hands on the wall, one on each side of her head. She'd never seen him look so fierce.

Fear and anticipation filled her, but she had no place to go.

"I think—" Jack said, his voice deeper than she'd ever heard it. "—we need to talk."

She might have spoken, maybe only moaned, but before she could make a sound, Jack crushed his mouth down on hers. She opened beneath the onslaught, still trying to protest, but his tongue swept inside and stole her words away. A moan burst in her throat and became embarrassingly loud as he pulled away.

"Put your hands on me," Jack ordered. "Now."

With a whimper, Josie spread both her hands on his chest. His shirt was cold with the rain, and so tight she felt every ripple of his muscles. His nipples were hard as iron beneath her fingers. When she touched them, he muttered a curse.

"Jack..."

"Shut up, Josie."

Her eyes widened, then narrowed. Jack was the only man who could talk to her like that without a punch in the gut for his efforts. Even so, she opened her mouth to tell him off. He stopped her with another kiss.

Her arms slid around his neck. His mouth molded to hers. Their tongues twined and twisted, dancing. After a minute, she felt him shivering against her and she became aware that her dry t-shirt had become damp.

She broke the kiss and heard the click of his teeth as they chattered.

"Jack, you're freezing!"

He didn't answer with words, just another kiss. His mouth was hot, if nothing else was. Josie put her hands to his waist and tugged his wet shirt from his pants. Their mouths remained locked as she lifted the shirt up his belly and over his chest. He lifted his arms to allow her to pull it over his head. They broke apart and rejoined, mouths meeting greedily. She dropped the shirt, forgotten, to the floor.

Josie put her hands on Jack's bare skin and felt the gooseflesh there. He shivered again when she made circles on his skin with her fingers. His skin warmed under her touch.

Jack put his hands to her waist and lifted her. The strength of his arms left her dizzy with arousal as he urged her, with a touch, to wrap her legs around him. Now her head was higher than his. She put her hands on his head, and the bristly stubble along his jaw scratched at her fingers.

The movement pushed her shirt above her thighs. She was bare beneath it. Jack groaned against her mouth as her dark red curls brushed his belly.

His hands slid down to cup her ass and hold her up. The wall was hard on her back, and Jack was even harder on her front. He pushed against her, and her clit rubbed the bare skin of his chest. She thought she might faint. His hands kneaded her ass, pulling her infinitesimally closer then pushing her back, just enough to keep the pressure building in her clit.

She didn't want to stop kissing. But lost in the sensations, Josie had to leave his mouth so she could gasp a breath. His mouth found her throat, and she let her head touch the wall behind her. His tongue swirled on her skin. He let her slip down a fraction of an inch, so now she pressed against the cold metal of his belt buckle. The new sensation on her heated flesh made her groan aloud.

One hand left her ass, but he was so strong he didn't let her drop any further. She felt his hands working at his belt. His pants clung to him from the wetness. Her senses reeling, Josie had time to think that they had reached the point of no return, only to be hampered by a stubborn pair of trousers that refused to be shucked.

She ought to have known better. Jack was too persistent to give up so easily. He pulled her against him so she was totally supported on his hands. He carried her from the hall, across the living room and into her bedroom.

Despite their mutual urgency, Jack didn't throw Josie onto the bed. Instead, with one hand beneath her ass and the other cradling her head, he laid her down as gently as if he were placing fine china. The subtle, tender gesture took her breath away without lessening her need.

This is crazy.

He crawled up the bed over her, and as he lifted his hips she helped him push down the wet and clinging material. The pants, briefs inside them, stuck on the smoothness of his ass, but Josie pushed and Jack pulled. The fabric bunched and caught on his boots, and he bent to unlace them with impatient fingers. The string knotted, and with a curse, he tore the laces open. With a kick of one foot against the other, he finally rid himself of his pants and slid back over her to kiss her again.

He lay between her thighs as they kissed. Josie's legs parted to accommodate him. She waited, aching for him to enter her. Jack pulled away. Startled, Josie opened her eyes.

Jack moved his mouth down to the pulse beating in her throat. His tongue traced circles on her skin. He nipped along the edge of her shoulder, exposed by the neckline of her too-large shirt. He continued over the curve of her breast, pausing to suckle a moment through the damp fabric. Josie pushed upward to allow him greater access, but Jack had already moved down over the slope of her belly, across her naked hip, bared by the lifted hem of her shirt. His lips traveled down her thigh, nuzzling the soft downy hairs she didn't bother to shave. Then over where she needed him to be, where she'd dreamed of him being for so long...so fucking long....

She was suddenly overjoyed she'd taken the time to shower.

Jack put one hand on each of her inner thighs and supported himself on his elbows between her legs. He dipped his head to lick her with a finesse she'd always known he'd have. Back and forth, up and down, then settling into a small, circular pattern that took her to the edge within moments.

As if he were completely attuned to her body, Jack backed off. Josie sighed a protest. He touched her, lightly, with one hand. Her clit pulsed beneath his touch.

She looked down to see him watching her, a question in his eyes. Josie nodded almost imperceptibly, giving him permission. Her heart swelled as he bent to love her with his tongue again. This was Jack between her legs, her Jack, her friend and now, at last, her lover.

There was no guilt, no shame. She'd loved him for years as a man she could count on for anything. He'd been there through tears and laughter, held her hand through times of trouble, sent her flowers on her birthday when nobody else remembered. Tomorrow might bring regret, but at this moment, Josie gave herself up to the feelings she'd been hiding for too damn long.

Jack's breath sent a shiver crawling up her. She was going to come again. After her orgasm on the dance floor, she didn't think she'd have been able, but her body knew better than her mind. Desire fluttered within her, and she fought it, wanted to make this last and last.

Barry had always refused to go down on her. He said he didn't like the smell, the taste, and the way her pubic hair felt on his tongue. He'd been insistent about blowjobs, though. In the last month of their six-month relationship, Josie giving Barry head was the only sex they'd had.

Now she pressed herself into the softness of the bed and gave herself up to the feeling of Jack's mouth and hands on her. He was as skilled at cunnilingus as he was at dancing. He knew how to lead her, how to bring her close, then soften the touch so she didn't go over. Her mind-blowing climax on the dance floor hadn't totally relieved her frustration, but it had decreased it to manageability. Now she was content to ride the waves of sensation flooding her without urging herself to immediate climax.

Jack slipped a finger inside her, then two. He slid in and out in perfect rhythm with the slow, steady pressure of his tongue. She let out a cry and lifted her hips, asking without words for more. He gave it to her. He curved his fingers inside her to press against the spot just behind her pubic bone. She felt a pressure, almost a burning, then he flicked her clit lightly with her tongue.

Josie's entire body clenched. Her inner muscles contracted around his fingers. Her clit pulsed and throbbed...but she didn't come. Not yet. It would take only the slightest amount of pressure and she'd go over the edge, but Jack had stopped moving.

He pulled his fingers free, slowly, then kissed his way back up her belly, her breasts, then to her throat and finally her mouth again. His body covered her, and she felt him nudge at her opening.

"Wait," Josie breathed.

In the dim light of her bedroom, she couldn't see the flecks of gold she knew were in Jack's eyes. She pushed his shoulder gently until he rolled off her and onto his back. She'd waited too long for this to happen for it to be over so soon. Besides, she'd longed for Jack's cock in her mouth as much as she'd wanted to make love to him.

He stretched one arm behind his head to support it as he looked at her. The lines of his body flowed like sculpture. He was pure perfection.

Josie let her eyes feast hungrily on him. She knew every inch of Jack's body already, but she'd never allowed herself to look at it like this.

Josie reached to touch the smooth, hard contours of his chest, and her fingers brushed the soft, scattered dark hairs there. Down her fingers trailed on the fine line of black hair along the muscled lines of his belly to join the thick curly pelt of his pubic region. She stopped there, unable to look away from his erection.

Josie had shared a bed and a bathroom with Jack more times than she could count. They'd vacationed together, crashed on each other's couches, even lived together briefly for a time when Jack had been between jobs. Even so, she'd never seen him this way.

Jack's cock was something of a private joke between them. The monster, the beast, the drill. Josie had no illusions about Jack's proportions. Unlike a lot of men whose muscles outstripped their equipment, Jack's cock was as large as everything else about him.

"The beast," she murmured, and stroked a finger along his length. "The drill. Mercy, Jack, I'm surprised you haven't killed anyone with this yet."

To her surprise, he didn't respond with a witty comeback. His dick pulsed under her fingers. She stroked him again, and the low, soft sigh that escaped him echoed in the throb of her clit.

"How long has it been?" she asked him.

"A year."

His answer so shocked her she involuntarily squeezed his erection. "The hell you say!"

With a wry grin that was a mere shadow of his normal thigh-spreading smile, Jack put his hand over hers. "Not so hard, Josie."

"Sorry." She loosened her fingers and bent to kiss the tip of his penis.

Jack cursed and covered his eyes with his arm. Josie let her fingers slide down to cup the weight of his balls. His reaction endeared him to her even more.

"A whole year?" She asked. "Jack, why?"

He scrubbed at his face before looking at her. "Because I couldn't find anyone I wanted to be with more than I wanted to be with you."

Now her shock made her scoot back on the bed. "What?"

Jack sat up and took her hands in his. Naked, he faced her across the bed, his expression more serious than she'd ever seen it. "Josie, don't you know how long it's been you?"

She shook her head, tears sparking at her eyes and burning in her throat. Jack lifted one hand to cup her cheek.

She swiped at her face, embarrassed by her show of emotion.

"Why didn't you say anything?" she asked.

"You were with Barry. And before that... Hell, Josie, you know me. I'd never wanted to get tied down before. I didn't want you to think it was just part of The Game. I didn't want to lose you."

Josie blinked and looked at Jack's face. His hand slid from her cheek to her shoulder. She put her hand on his arm to pull him closer.

They kissed, softly, then harder. He captured her neck with his hand and rocked her toward him. Josie splayed her hands on the bare heat of his chest.

This time, spurred by Jack's admittance of how long it had been since he'd been with anyone, she took charge. Josie slid her tongue along the curve of his jaw, down his throat, to his shoulder. She pushed him back onto the pillows again then let her lips make a trail to the hard point of his nipple. Her tongue swirled around the tip, and she suckled lightly. Jack's hips jerked, and she curled her fingers around his shaft again. Lightly, softly, she stroked his cock in time to the gentle sucking of his nipple.

He tangled his hand in her hair, loosening it from the ponytail. The strands fell across her face and shoulders, along the neckline of her borrowed tee shirt. Impatiently, Josie sat up to tug off the shirt then bent back to her task.

From one nipple to the other, she concentrated on pleasing him. After a moment, without ceasing her teasing strokes, she kissed the ridges of his six-pack abs. She followed the slightly jutting edge of his hipbone, and paused to sink her teeth into his skin just enough to make him mutter another curse. He pushed himself into her hand, urging for her to stroke him harder. She didn't. She had Jack at her mercy now, and she wasn't about to let him take control.

Josie left his hip and went down to the perfection of his ankle. She kissed it. Licked it. Let her mouth slide up the bulge of his calf, then to his knee. She kissed the top of his thigh and ran her tongue along it, all the while stroking him firmly, but slowly.

He strained upward into her hand, but she refused to quicken the pace. She relished the way the thin skin of his cock slipped beneath her fingers, and the heat it gave off. She stopped to toy gently with the head of his penis, finding the first slippery drops of pre-come and smoothing them down to lubricate him.

Her own hand slipped between her legs to caress her still-aroused clit. She didn't stroke herself, afraid she'd send herself into another orgasm, but the light touch kept her close to the edge. She moved her hips against the cup of her palm, teasing herself as she teased him.

At last, she took pity on him. She didn't bother with teasing anymore, simply lowered her mouth on his cock all the way to its root. Her lips enclosed him. She relaxed her throat to take him in all the way, and his low oath of surprise was worth the effort.

Jack's cock nudged the back of her throat and she slid out, adding a little extra suction at the tip. Josie had never been fond of monstrous cocks with veins and ugly purple heads. Jack's penis was as lovely and perfect as the rest of his body—large, but not grotesque. She slid her mouth again along his entire length, her saliva leaving a glistening trail.

She added the use of her hand at the base of his erection. She sucked and stroked in tandem. Josie moved between Jack's legs to give herself better access to his balls, which she stroked with her other hand. She stroked her thumb down the small ridge of flesh on the underside of his testicles, then found the smooth spot at the base of his scrotum. She pressed gently, in counterpoint to sliding him in and out of her mouth. As she did, he surged beneath her and bucked so fiercely she lost her grip.

"Josie!"

For a moment, she thought she'd hurt him. Then she realized, by the way his balls tightened and his cock lengthened, that she'd aroused him instead.

"Nobody," he managed to say. "Damn. Nobody ever..."

"Poor Jack," Josie murmured. She swirled her tongue on only the head of his penis. "You've been wasting your time with the wrong girls."

The ocean-like taste of his pre-come slipped on her tongue. Her belly clenched at the sweetness. Josie rubbed her thighs together as she continued sucking him, building her own tension.

"You have to stop."

She paused to shake her head. "No."

"Please, Josie. I want to make love to you."

Josie looked up at him. His eyes glittered in the light from the street lamp outside the bedroom window. He licked his lips, no sign of teasing on his face.

"I'm going to come," Jack said. "It's been too long. You feel too good."

She stroked his balls again, and his cock twitched under her palm. She thought of how they'd danced, and how good that first orgasm had felt, after so long without one. They'd have time to make love together later. For now, this was her gift to him.

She stroked again with both hands. Jack said nothing, maybe unable to speak. He'd raised both hands to grab the pillow behind his head, and now his forearm shadowed his face again.

Without a second thought, Josie bent and slid him into her mouth again. This time, she moved faster, sucked harder, until he thrust urgently into her mouth.

His cock swelled impossibly huge, nearly enough to choke her. Josie pressed her thumb again to the sweet spot, felt the answering throb deep inside him, and Jack came.

He'd reached down to hold her head, and now his fingers clutched so hard in her hair she almost cried out. He thrust upward and she took him in as far as she could. The taste of him so aroused her that her clit pulsed in a mini-climax that had her not-quite-coming.

As if he realized he was pulling her hair hard enough to hurt, Jack untangled his fingers. "Oh, my God."

Josie couldn't help it. She laughed. She'd never laughed in bed before, not with a lover, anyway, but it felt so good to do so she laughed even harder. She kissed Jack's semi-erect penis through her giggles, then crawled up the bed to lie beside him.

He rolled onto his side to look at her. "You laughing at me?"

She touched his mouth. "Not at you, baby. With you."

She'd called him baby. Heat crept up her throat to paint her cheeks. Jack grinned widely.

"Baby?"

Josie ducked her head and pushed at his chest. "Shut up..."

"Baby?" Jack asked again. His fingers found the ticklish spot just under her ribs, and she writhed beneath his touch. "Josephine Levine, you called me baby."

"Shut up!" Josie managed to gasp from between her giggles, as he tickled her some more.

Jack rolled on top of her and pinned her arms above her head. "I like it."

Then he was kissing her again, and her laughter turned to a moan of pleasure.

For such a large man, he should have crushed her into the bed. Josie didn't mind Jack's weight on her at all. She parted her legs, and her slickness rubbed his lower stomach. Her clitoris rubbed on his skin. Jack let go of one of her hands and slipped his hand beneath her rear to press her harder against him.

He kissed her without stopping, but she had no trouble breathing. He breathed in, and she breathed out. Like snorkeling, like dreaming, like flying. How could she have ever breathed without Jack beside her to help her along?

"Josie...."

Somehow, she managed to speak. "Yeah?"

"I'm...I don't...have anything."

Josie hesitated, pushing him back gently so she could look at his face. "You mean a condom?"

"I don't have one of those, either. But I mean, I'm clean. Everything tested out okay. And it's been a year." Jack brushed his mouth against hers. "Just wanted you to know."

Josie had condoms in her night stand, of course. She was on the pill but wouldn't fuck without another form of protection, at least not with someone else. But this was Jack, and if he told her he was safe, she believed him.

"I'm good too," she whispered against his mouth. "After the breakup, I got a full screen."

She always did, which Jack would've known. She pulled away again to look into his eyes. He lifted her, urging her to move her hips in small circles that pressed her clit against him. With a move she wouldn't have believed if she hadn't felt it, he lifted his hips just enough to bring his returning erection against her center. Jack met her languid thrusts and rubbed his cock along her folds. Not in her, just on her, coating his shaft with her wetness until he slid along her without friction. His balls pressed lightly against her with every thrust.

She wanted him inside her. She didn't think she could stand it if he didn't slide into her, now, hard. Jack wasn't done teasing her though. Still capturing her mouth with his, he stroked against her until she shuddered on the edge of orgasm.

Jack lifted her chin with his finger so she had to meet his eyes. "Are you sure?"

She nodded. "Yes. I'm more sure about this than I've been about anything."

Jack pulled her to him for another kiss. His arm went around her back, his hand cupped her head, and he lowered her gently to the pillow. He covered her body with his. The heat of his erection pushed at her opening, and Josie lifted her hips to help him in.

He pushed himself into her all the way. He stretched her, filled her. Completed her. Jack kissed her as he moved, slowly at first, then into a steady rhythm that had her lifting her hips to meet his thrusts. Everything about being with Jack just felt right.

He rolled slowly to one side, pulling her with him until she was on top. She rocked against him, loving the way her clit rubbed his hard stomach as he thrust inside her. The position gave her the freedom to control the movements. She rose on her knees and put one hand on each side of his head. Now she could bend to kiss him, while moving herself along his entire length.

Jack ran his hands down her back and cupped her ass. He didn't force the pace, but let her go as fast or slow as she wanted. He arched upward, into her, as she slid down then let hips roll back when she lifted up. They moved in perfect tandem, just like when they danced.

"It might take me a while," he confided, as she moved her hips in a circular motion.

Josie grinned and sank down on him completely, holding him inside her warmth. "You have someplace you have to be?"

Jack shook his head. "Hell, no."

"Me neither. We have all night." Josie sat up straight and braced herself on her heels next to Jack's thighs.

"Josie, you can't last all night," Jack teased. He slipped one hand from her ass to press his thumb against her clitoris. "I'm going to get you off in about another minute."

Josie's only reply was a soft sigh. She let her head fall back, reeling with the sensation of his thumb pressing in counterpoint to her long, slow strokes. He was probably right, but did she care? She felt like she could come a hundred times tonight. Set some sort of world record.

"What are you thinking?" he asked, bringing her back to reality.

"About you," Josie said, and leaned to kiss him fully. "About how glad I am I have you."

Jack put his hands to her waist and stopped her from moving. She looked at him curiously as he pulled her off his cock and pushed her gently to the bed.

"Get on your hands and knees," he told her.

The words sent a bolt of fire shooting through her. She did as he told her. The pillow was soft beneath her cheek, and she clutched it.

Behind her, Jack put one hand to his cock and guided himself into the entrance she offered. At this angle, he filled her so deeply she didn't think she'd be able to stand it. He waited for her to move against him, and when she did, he set up a steady pace that had her gasping in minutes.

She was so close to the edge, but still not quite there. She needed some more direct stimulation on her clit, but Jack seemed determined to tease her. Josie pushed back against him, letting him fill her. She'd never come in this position before, usually because it didn't provide the kind of pressure she needed on her clit.

Now she concentrated on the feeling of him sliding into her. The way he gave his cock a little twist with each thrust. The way he gave a series of short, swift strokes followed by a pattern of deep, slow thrusts. His cock swelled within her, stretching her further.

Her clitoris ached to be touched. Josie arched her back to push herself onto Jack harder. With every thrust, her clit throbbed harder and she got closer to coming, but it wasn't... quite...enough...

Then Jack did it. He slipped one hand around to put his first two fingers directly on her swollen clit. Josie cried out and shuddered. She was so wet his fingers slid over and around her engorged clit like he'd covered them in oil. She clutched the pillow harder and pushed herself up on her hands.

Jack took her clit between his thumb and finger, and pinched gently. The sensation was so new and so unaccustomed it shocked her into an orgasm unlike any other she'd ever had. A fierce, sharp burst of pleasure jabbed her directly beneath his tweaking fingers, then built again into another, fiercer burst. She had no aftershocks, no rippling contractions, and no sense of the pleasure fading, as she usually did. Just one burst after another, like a series of fireworks.

"Jack!"

She shuddered and wriggled beneath him. He slipped out of her, and she cried in protest, even as his fingers still kept up their gentle pressure. Another burst of orgasm built and crested. He took his hand away and pushed her onto her back.

Jack slid into her again, to the hilt. She slipped her arms around his back to hold him closer then hooked her feet around his calves. He put his hands under her ass to tilt her further onto his cock. The angle opened her more and sent her spiraling into a final orgasm.

Waves of climax rolled over her. Her nipples tightened. She felt as though everything in her body, blood and air, was pulling inward, downward, into the tiny button of her clitoris. Tighter, tighter, drawing together like a fist clenching. She let out a low, small cry, and said his name over and over.

All at once, she opened like a flower beneath the springtime sun. Ecstasy shot from her center and radiated through her entire body. She rose, she flew, she fell apart, and came back together.

Josie lost her breath with the intensity of her climax. Stars sparkled in her vision. She gasped and writhed, and pulled Jack against her harder. He dipped his head to fasten his mouth where her neck met her shoulder. The sting of his bite sent another wave of pleasure rocketing through her. The aftershocks built until she came again, less intensely but no less pleasurably than the first.

He kissed the bite he'd made. His thrusts became faster and more ragged. His fingers gripped the softness of her buttocks and he pulled her against him tighter.

Josie, still flying, clutched his back and nuzzled his neck. Jack moaned. She replied with a small, encouraging noise of her own.

"Josie." He panted her name, and the end of it trailed into another groan.

He shuddered. She felt him beat beside inside of her, rapidly, like the flutter of a moth on a windowpane. She held him tighter as he gave one final thrust and fully buried himself inside her.

They stayed without moving for a few long moments, until he rolled to her side. He pulled her close, so she pillowed her head on his chest. Josie put her hand over his heart, which slowly ceased its rampant thumping and returned to a normal pace.

There seemed to be so much to say, but no words adequate to say it. She contented herself with silence and the sound of his heart in her ear. He stroked her hair and held her close.

"I thought you didn't like redheads," she said drowsily, as sleep began to overtake her.

"You should know me better than that. I love a redhead." Jack toyed with a strand of her auburn hair, then squeezed her. He gave a low, throaty chuckle and another of his heart-stopping, thigh-spreading grins. "Baby."

OPENING THE DOOR

ONE

Josie woke to the sensation of something wet on her toes. Reflexively, she shot out her foot beneath the covers. It connected with something. Hard.

"Damn, Josie!"

Jack threw off the covers and appeared at the foot of the bed, rubbing his head. "What're you doing?"

Josie giggled and reached for him. "Sorry, baby. You startled me."

Jack grumbled, but let her kiss the spot she'd wounded before curling along her body and nestling his head in the curve of her shoulder. "I thought I'd surprise you.'

"You certainly did."

Waking up with Jack was a pleasure Josie still couldn't quite get used to. It had been seven months of bliss since they'd taken the leap from friendship to love, and there still wasn't a day she didn't look over at him sleeping beside her and send up gratitude.

Sunday morning. No place to go, nothing to do, a warm, comfortable bed and the man she loved beside her. She couldn't ask for anything better than that. Josie let her eyes drift closed again as the rhythm of Jack's breathing soothed her back to sleep.

In another moment, she felt his hand rest on the curve of her stomach. He bunched his fingers on the cotton of the oversize T-shirt she'd worn to bed and pulled the material up over her thighs. With the covers tangled around her ankles, the air was slightly chilly on her skin.

She mumbled a protest, but his kiss on her neck stopped her. She smiled, eyes still closed. He was going to surprise her again.

Jack rubbed small circles on her bare belly with the flat of his palm. His hand was so large it covered her nearly from side to side. His fingers skimmed the edge of her cotton bikini panties.

He slipped lower, over the soft cotton barrier, and cupped her. She shifted her thighs to give him better access. She didn't open her eyes—the better to lose herself in the sensations he was giving her. His fingertip found the small bump of her clit and he began to stroke it in the same, slow circles he'd used on her stomach.

Josie sighed. Jack kissed her neck. His breath was hot on her skin. The tip of his tongue caressed her briefly before she felt the nip of his teeth.

The pattern of his strokes had her on the edge within a minute or two, but he didn't get her off right then. He knew her too well for that. Jack liked to tease. He backed off, changed the rhythm, made the strokes longer and up and down instead of the steady circles he knew she adored. His hand slipped lower, further down the now-damp crotch of her panties. He pressed the heel of his hand against her and let his fingers play along the soft flesh of her inner thigh.

Still, Josie feigned sleep. She knew Jack knew she was awake. It was just more fun to play this way, to see how long it would take before she couldn't stop herself from moaning and reaching for him.

Up again went his hand, this time to dip below the elastic of her panties and slide through the curls beneath. His fingertip found her swollen clit, but he bypassed it to tickle her folds, and press her opening. He didn't push his finger inside, though she waited in breathless anticipation. He smoothed his finger along her flesh. Taunting her.

Josie shifted again and opened herself more to his exploration. Jack didn't take the hint. He kept up slow, gentle stroking, pausing every now and then to lightly touch her clit.

It was driving her crazy, and he knew it. Josie tilted her hips the next time he slipped down, and he gave her what she wanted. His finger slid inside her. First the tip, then the full length. His thumb found her clit and pressed in gentle counterpoint to the slow sliding of his finger.

Josie moaned. Jack had won the game. She didn't care. Losing was actually more fun.

"Tell me what you want," he said.

"Don't you know by now?"

His deep chuckle against her neck made her nipples peak and her pussy contract. Josie put her hand on top of his head and let the scruff of his close-cropped hair scratch at her palm. He nestled his head into her shoulder and curled along her body. She opened her eyes and cocked her head to look at him.

"I know," Jack said. "I just want to hear you say it."

In all their years of friendship, Josie had never known of Jack's fetish for explicit talk. They'd shared a lot of secrets, but until she became his lover, this was one he'd never told.

It still surprised her, how just her speaking could get him so hot. How the tone of her voice, her choice of words, could turn him on as much as her mouth or her hands. She'd never dreamed she'd find as much pleasure in talking as she did in making love, but there it was. Loving Jack had opened up a lot of new doors for her.

"Put your mouth on me," Josie said. Jack's muffled groan made her laugh, until he did as she asked and the laugh became a squeak.

His hands slipped beneath her to cup her ass and he lifted her toward his mouth. His tongue swiped her lightly then swirled on her clit for the briefest of seconds. His breath was hot.

"Put your tongue on my clit."

It was still difficult to speak aloud sometimes. Telling him what she wanted and needed sounded like dialogue from a bad porn movie. Jack would never laugh at her. He loved it when she talked dirty. But it still took Josie a lot of effort to let go. She tried again, distracted by Jack's tongue swirling on her button.

"Put your finger inside me."

"Put your finger inside me, what?"

Again, Josie let out a giggle that became half a gasp when he complied. "Put your finger inside me, Jack."

She was the one telling him what to do, but that didn't mean he'd given up control. He slid his finger inside while he kept up the same steady rhythm on her clit with his tongue. The pleasure mounted. She forgot to breathe. She also forgot to speak.

Jack's lips moved against her flesh, sending another ripple of pleasure through her. "Tell me what you want, Josie."

It was hard to speak, but she found her voice. It had gone low and husky. "Lick me. Harder. Right there..." Her voice broke as the first waves of climax began to wash over her.

Jack pulled away. His finger stilled. He breathed on her. The sensation was not quite enough to send her over the edge. She remembered to breathe.

"Are you going to come?"

She barely had the air to giggle again, but she did. "Hell, yeah."

She tilted her head to glance down at him, expecting him to be smiling. He was staring at her seriously. "Good."

"Jack?"

"Because I want to make you come so hard you scream my name, Josie, and then I'm going to slide up your body and fuck you until you come again."

Though he liked her to be explicit, Josie had never heard Jack talking dirty before. All at once she understood the appeal. Hearing him say aloud what he was thinking made her pussy flutter. Her clit pulsed but didn't begin the final beating spasm of orgasm. Not quite.

Josie hovered on the edge of coming for what felt like an eternity. One kiss, one stroke, one breath and she'd be over the edge, but Jack gave her none of those. She found herself lifting her hips toward him in a silent appeal.

"Tell me what you want, Josie."

"Use your mouth on me," she managed to whisper. The darkness behind her closed eyes swirled with colored lights that moved with the thud of her heart. She imagined she could feel her blood pumping through her body, in her chest, her belly, between her legs. She waited, tense, for his mouth to touch her.

His finger moved slowly, excruciatingly slowly. He twisted it inside her, then slipped another inside to stretch her. And still he didn't touch her clit, though she felt the burning puff of his breath there, where she needed it most.

Her mouth opened, her head tilted back on the pillows. Every fiber of her being strained toward him, toward release. "Please, Jack."

"Please what?"

"Please fuck me with your tongue and make me come, or I'm going to slap you silly!" The words tumbled out of her in a rush, full of need and passion, but also the exasperated humor she knew he expected.

His hand moved. He brushed her tight clit with his lips, then took it between them and tugged ever–so-gently while she gasped and cried out his name. Her head tossed on the pillow. He fucked her faster with his fingers, in and out, while his lips continued to tug softly on her swollen flesh. She'd stayed so long on the verge of orgasm that her body now stuttered in its response. She was strung high-wire tight. Josie's hips rolled and her thighs trembled.

Just a bit more penetration, a little more pressure, and she'd come so hard she'd scream his name, just like he wanted. If she had the breath to do it, that was.

Jack flicked his tongue along her folds but once again bypassed her need, damn him. He swirled around the hood of her clit but didn't touch the button within. Another swipe of his tongue along the opening to her pussy left her shuddering with a delayed climax. His fingers moved in and out, twisting inside her. He curled them, found the spongy texture of her g-spot and pressed it.

She was going over. Now, at last, his tongue found her clit and he no longer teased her. Jack's tongue stabbed at her with a pressure she'd have found intolerable in a less-aroused state, but now she screamed with the ecstasy of it.

Her entire pelvis flooded with sensation. Everything drew in toward that one small spot...then exploded.

He eased off, slid his fingers out, pressed his lips to her pulsing clit and held her until the final raging spasm passed through her. He kissed her gently, then slid up the bed and cradled her in his arms.

Josie couldn't speak for what felt like quite a while. Then she managed a feeble, "Whoa."

Jack's dark eyes glinted. "I take it that was good."

"Don't fish for compliments, Jack." She put a hand up to stroke his close-shaven head. "But, yeah, that was good."

"That's only the first part," he reminded. "Don't forget what else I said I was going to do to you."

Even after the force of her climax, his words made her pussy twitch.

"Are you ready for me?" he asked.

"I'm always ready for you." Her voice was teasing, but actually, she wasn't quite certain she was. Her head still swam and her heart still pounded. She took a few deep breaths as her body calmed.

Josie could usually tell within minutes if she'd be able to have another orgasm. Her cunt didn't stop trembling and her clit still buzzed. In the aftermath of what she'd just experienced, though, her entire body still hummed with bliss. Jack put a hand on her mound and simply held her without stroking or pressure. She throbbed under his touch, and Josie took in another deep breath.

"I love you, Josie." Jack whispered the words in her ear as he nuzzled her. His fingers made a lazy, drifting pattern on her skin.

"I love you, too." She sighed with contentment.

Jack rolled on top of her and rested for a moment on his forearms. His cock nudged her opening, and he thrust a bit into her wetness to lubricate his entrance. The tip of him stretched her before he withdrew, slightly changed the angle and seated himself fully inside her with one smooth thrust.

They fit like puzzle pieces. Josie lifted her hips to draw him deeper. She ran her hands over the bulging muscles of his arms, then up to his tautly sculptured shoulders and back. Jack had been blessed with a naturally fit physique that took little work to maintain. She hated him for it when he was eating ice cream and she was nibbling rice cakes. She loved him for it now.

She drew up her knees and hooked her heels over his ass as he slid in and out. She loved the feeling of his muscles working as he moved. She thought he might be urgent to finish, since she'd already had her orgasm, but Jack's rhythm was as steady and slow as the rest of his lovemaking.

They rocked together for a while. Josie floated in a sensuous reverie. Without the pressure to come before he did, she relaxed and opened herself to the feelings she normally missed when concentrating solely on the sensations in her clit.

She bore down as he moved inside her and her pussy gripped him. She concentrated on the feeling of her inner walls hugging his thick cock and how he felt inside her. Sex usually focused mostly on her clit because that's where she needed the stimulation to come. Now, she focused on the other feelings.

Jack lowered himself onto her, and she welcomed his weight by curling her arms around his back. She smoothed her hands down the firm lines, then gripped the curving firmness of his ass with both hands.

Her breasts tingled beneath the pressure of his chest on hers. Her nipples stiffened and rubbed against his as he moved back and forth. His teeth nipped at her neck and throat, and his tongue came after to lick the spots he'd nibbled.

Sweat made their bodies slick, allowing them to move like oiled machinery against one another. His cock slid without effort inside her. The rim of his pelvis rubbed her still-buzzing clit, and desire began to build once more.

As much as she adored the feeling of Jack on top of her, he was a big man. Lovemaking that left her breathless was one thing, but not being able to breathe was another. Josie pushed at Jack's hips and he rolled onto his side. Now he thrust into her from the side, while she lay on her back, her left leg beneath his thigh and her right overtop his. She could breathe. Better still, the new position allowed her to reach down and stroke his balls with one hand while she rubbed her clitoris with the other.

When she touched his sac, Jack moaned her name. Josie smiled, pleased with herself. She'd discovered another benefit to not striving so fiercely for orgasm. She got to pay more attention to the things that got Jack off. She moved her fingers back and forth along the small ridge of flesh at the base of his scrotum. She found the spot that beat along with his heart, and pressed it gently.

"That's good," Jack said. "Right there."

Hearing him speak, his breath ragged, made her swallow hard. His big hand rubbed her belly, then slipped lower to caress her clit while he continued to thrust.

They had become a tangle of arms and legs, a pretzel of pleasure. Josie smiled at the thought and opened herself further to his hand and prick, while she pressed gently on his sweet spot.

He was going to come. And surprisingly, she was too. Josie tilted her pelvis upward beneath his fingers, and he penetrated her so deeply she felt his cockhead nudging her cervix. What might have been painful became just one more burst of sensation. At this angle, Jack's shaft rubbed on her g-spot. Bliss began to radiate from the spot in slow, warm waves and, after a moment, the sharper, more biting sparks of orgasm burst in her clit. She cried out.

Jack shuddered and thrust, hard. Josie pushed firmly on the spot under his balls. It beat beneath her fingers, echoing the spasms of his cock as he shot his load deep within her. She let up on the pressure, then pushed again. Jack gave a startled moan and his dick throbbed anew inside her.

Josie's passage clenched down on him, then relaxed. She put her hand on Jack's to stop him from stroking her sensitized flesh any more. Her hips jerked in the final spasms, and she sighed contentedly.

"Where did you learn that?" Jack asked solemnly, after a moment of silence.

"What do you mean?" She rolled her head to look at him.

"Felt like I came twice when you touched me like that."

Josie smiled. "I read it in some magazine while I was at the doctor's office."

Jack slipped out of her and they adjusted themselves to lie together on the bed. "Damn, Josie. I might have to get you a subscription to that magazine."

She laughed and caressed his shoulder. "I'm glad you liked it."

"Did *you* come again?"

She still wasn't used to a man who actually bothered to ask if she'd been satisfied once, much less again. "Of course I did."

Jack snorted, but looked pleased. "Of course."

"Listen, Jack." Josie turned on her side to cuddle next to him. "It would've been okay if I didn't."

He slipped an arm beneath her head and drew her to his chest. "I just want to make you happy."

Josie hugged him as tightly as she could. "How could you think you don't?"

His deep, rumbling laughter reverberated through her chest. "I guess you're right, considering your last boyfriend..."

She swatted him. "Shut up."

Jack stretched out his hands behind his head and gave her the grin she knew so well. "I'm just saying..."

She gave a mock shudder. "Well, don't."

He squeezed her. "You can go ahead and thank me for taking you away from all that any time, baby."

Josie rolled her eyes and swung her legs out of bed as the phone rang. "I'll bow down before you and worship at your feet later, master."

"Hey, I like the sound of that."

She laughed at him and picked up the phone from the bedside table. "Jack and Josie's den of iniquity. Oh, hi, Mom."

Jack began to laugh and Josie through a pillow at him. "Nothing," she said in response to her mother's inquiry. She turned her back to ignore Jack, who had started to make faces.

"How are you, honey?" her mother asked.

Somehow, Josie didn't think her mother would appreciate hearing she'd just had the greatest sex of her life. "Fine. How about you?"

Her mother began to chatter about life back in Philadelphia, but Josie was having a hard time concentrating because Jack had begun to lick her bare back. She wriggled away from him, and silently cursed their corded phone, which didn't allow her to move far enough out of his reach.

"...home for the holiday?"

Her mother had paused, waiting for an answer. Josie suddenly realized she was expected to give one. "Um. Yeah. I hadn't thought much about it."

Jack sat up and raised his eyebrows at her. "Holiday?" he mouthed, and Josie nodded.

"You *are* going to make it this year, aren't you?" Her mother didn't sound worried. Josie always went home for the holidays. "Your brother and sister are coming. We'll have Uncle Marty and Aunt Bea, of course, and Dad's cousin Bernie. Oh, and the Golds are coming up from Florida! It'll be a full house."

"The Golds?"

Jack's eyes widened. Josie shrugged. Her mother sighed, acting long-suffering, but clearly in her element.

"I told Francine and Ben it had been too long since we got together. They're coming for the whole week. You'll make sure Jack comes, too, won't you?"

"I think Jack's going to have to talk to his parents about that," Josie said, for his benefit, not her mother's.

Jack made a face and clutched his heart, then fell back on the bed. He twitched like a man in the throes of death, then popped up his head to grin at her. "Of course I'll go."

"Jack says of course he'll come, Mom. If you didn't bully him into it, he knows his mother would."

Her mom tutted. "Francine's never bullied that boy in his life. He's spoiled rotten."

"And you love him like he's your own son," Josie said, while Jack made another simpering face and blew kisses at the phone.

"I've known him since he was in diapers. How could I

not love him?" Ava Levine laughed. "How're the new living arrangements?"

"Fine." Josie bit her lip and turned her back on Jack again. "Great. The new place is a lot bigger."

Her mother's sigh sounded like a tornado even through the phone lines. "And the dating situation?"

"Mom..."

"What? A mother can't ask her only single child if there's a chance she might someday settle down?"

Josie pictured her mother tossing her perfectly manicured hands in the air. She kept her face turned from Jack. "Mom, don't push."

"Who's pushing? I'm just asking. What about Jack? Is he seeing anyone nice? Francine said he hasn't brought anyone home to meet them in ages."

Josie took a deep breath. "Mom, there's something—"

"Oh, doll, your dad just got in. I need to get him to run to the store with me. Love to Jack!"

Just like that, her mother rang off. Josie put the phone back in its cradle and rubbed her temples. Her mother was a force of nature not to be trifled with.

"You didn't tell them yet, did you?"

She met Jack's accusing face. "They know we're living together. I just let them have the idea it's like before."

"Roommates."

Josie shrugged and bit her lip again. "Yes. Jack, you know my parents. They'd plotz if they thought I was living with a man...I mean living in sin with a man."

Jack harrumphed and sat up against the headboard, his arms crossed on his chest. "Your parents love me."

"Sure they do. As my friend. As the son of their best friends. But as my lover?" Josie shuddered, with no mockery this time. "Can you imagine?"

"Josephine Levine, are you ashamed of me?" Jack asked sternly.

For one minute she thought he was really insulted, but then she looked closer at the twinkle in his eyes. "Have you told *your* parents?"

He had the grace to look shame-faced. "Hell, no! Can you imagine what my mother would say?"

Josie let her head fall back and a deep sigh escape. "Home for the holiday. Oh. My. God."

Jack pulled her back down beside him. "C'mon. It might be fun."

Josie loved her family, her siblings, her nieces and nephews. She loved her parents, too. But the thought of spending an entire week with them...in one house... She let out a groan that had nothing to do with sex.

"Fun is a relative term when it comes to my relatives."

"Don't forget my folks." Jack pitched his voice high and gave it a nasally accent. "Good Lawd, Jackie! When are you gonna settle down and make me a gramma, already?"

"Your mom needed more kids."

Jack was adopted. He laughed. "Don't I know it."

Francine Gold was the stereotypical Jewish Bubbe with white curly hair and a gold lamé track suit. Josie had always thought of her as a second mother. Which meant she completely understood how Jack felt.

"It's only four days," she said at last.

Jack hummed Darth Vader's theme song. "Four days with both our mothers. In one house."

"At least there'll be plenty of wine." Josie moaned and covered her eyes. "We'll be doing a mitzvah."

"Josie, this is more than just a good deed. This is like, automatic entry into the Book of Life."

She laughed at his exaggeration, then kissed him. "Distract me until then."

He raised an eyebrow at her. "Okay, but promise me you'll tell them before we get there."

"I will if you will."

Jack reached down and hooked his little finger around hers like they'd done when they were kids. "Pinky swear?"

"Pinky swear."

Jack pulled her on top of him and covered her face with kisses. "Let's get back to distracting each other."

TWO

The phone had been ringing off the hook all morning. Josie would have let voicemail take care of it, but that would only mean she'd need to return all the calls later, and later she wouldn't have time. She'd have to take a half day to get down to her parents' house before the holiday started, and she had tons of work to get done before then.

"Good morning. This is Josephine Levine." She expected one of her clients.

Instead, her mother's exasperated voice greeted her. "Josie! Thank goodness. I'm glad I caught you. I've been trying to reach you at the apartment for days!"

Guilt picked at Josie. Jack had kicked the phone off the hook while they'd been making love, and it had been two days before either of them realized nobody could get through. "You should've called my cell. We never answer the landline."

"What's the use of having it, then?"

Josie laughed. "I don't know, good point. You have my cell number, don't you?"

"Yes, I have it," her mother said. "I just didn't realize you wouldn't answer your other phone. Listen, Jojo, I'm going crazy here. Aunt Flo has nowhere to go for Passover this year, and Dad said she could come here. Of course, I don't mind. I love your Aunt Flo, but you know she won't come without Pansy and Apricot."

Josie winced at her mother's childhood nickname for her. "Mom. Breathe."

Ava sighed. "Those dogs are like Flo's children. I can't ask her to leave them home. But you know Bernie and his allergies, and Bea with her bad back. And with all the kids, where am I going to put them all?"

Josie smiled. Her mother didn't need her help. Her mother could have organized Attila the Hun's elephant-mounted hordes without batting an eyelash or breaking a nail. Josie tapped her pencil on the list of things she still needed to do before leaving work tomorrow. "Mom, I've got to go."

"But what about you? And Jack, too? We're going to be packed to the brim this holiday. Not that I mind, of course. You know I love a house full of people more than anything. But it's a lot of work, I don't mind telling you."

"Mom—"

"Our family is growing and growing." Ava paused significantly. "Your brother and sister are married, and now they have the kids—"

"Mom, enough." Josie took a deep breath. "There's something I have to tell you."

"So, tell me already?"

"Jack and I..." Josie paused. "Jack and I will be sleeping together."

"Josephine, you're a treasure. That'll solve all my problems. I'll put Aunt Flo in the back downstairs bedroom with the dogs. Bernie can go on the third floor and the kids in the playroom. Marty and Bea can take your old room, Seth and Rachael and the baby can stay in Seth's old room, and Miriam and Brice can stay in her old room. The Golds will go in the guest room. You and Jack will sleep in the basement. It's perfect!"

"No, Mom, I—"

"Later, doll. I have to run to the supermarket! I want to get some of that chopped liver your brother likes so much. See you tomorrow. You'll be here before dinner, right?"

"Right." Josie sighed and listened to the dial tone for a moment before putting the phone back in its cradle. Then she laughed. Most young women would have sent their parents into a tizzy by suggesting she'd sleep with a man she was bringing home. Her mother, on the other hand, was thanking her. Of course, if it had been any man other than Jack, her mother would have swooned.

But it was Jack. Josie tilted back in her desk chair, her eyes half-closed. She was in love with her best friend, and it was better than anything she'd ever dreamed of.

As children, they'd played tag and hide-and-seek. In high school, he'd been her date when soccer stud Kent Dillon dumped her the afternoon before the junior prom. She'd cried on his shoulder and he'd offered to beat up the guy who'd hurt her so badly. In college, he'd visited for weekends and sent her dorm-mates into a flirting frenzy. After that, they'd kept in touch regularly, never going more than a week or two without calling, and when he'd finally moved to Harrisburg to follow a job, they hadn't been apart for more than a few days at a time.

She'd spent more time with Jack than she ever had with

any boyfriend. She'd shared more with him. Given more of herself to him. Despite all that, becoming lovers had opened a side of him she'd never seen.

This morning she'd wakened to find a lacy black garter belt, crotchless panties and matching bra laid out on the bed beside her. Sexy, seamed stockings completed the ensemble, which had come with a note. **Wear me**. Josie liked nice underwear, but comfort usually came before fashion. She'd worn the lingerie anyway.

Now she shifted her thighs against one another and shivered at the sensation of her flesh so bare beneath her skirt. The garter belt was surprisingly comfortable, stretchy and soft instead of scratchy like she'd expected. The stockings were whisper-thin, and when she slid her legs together it felt like she was rubbing herself with silk.

Her phone rang. Startled, she thumped her chair back down solidly on the floor and picked it up. "Josephine Levine."

"Are you wearing them?"

Josie turned in her chair and locked her office door. "Yes."

Jack's deep rumble stroked her ear through the phone. "How do they feel?"

"Good." His voice sent a spear of desire straight to her crotchless clit. Josie put her feet up on the desk, and tilted her chair back again.

"I've been thinking about you all morning. I bet you look so hot."

Josie looked down at the black skirt she'd worn today. It was shorter than she normally chose for work, and the heels of her shoes a good two inches higher. "You know it, baby."

Jack gave a whispery groan that made her pulse pound. "Tell me."

"I'm wearing a silky blue blouse, open at the throat. My skirt comes to the middle of my thighs."

"Shoes?" He sounded hopeful, and Josie grinned.

"Black patent leather. Three inch heels. Ankle strap."

He made a soft sound like he was licking his lips, and Josie shifted in her chair to let her knees fall slightly apart. Jack sighed. She heard the crackle of static from his cell phone.

"Pull your skirt up so the tops of your stockings show."

She did. "Are you driving?"

"I'm on my way to a sales call. Don't ruin the mood."

She laughed, loving that even the sexiest moments between them were filled with humor. "The tops of these stockings are lace."

"I know. Tell me about the panties. I bet your pretty pink clit is showing right now, isn't it? Is it standing up for me?"

Oh, he was a master at talking dirty. Josie had a lot to learn from him. His words had taken her breath, but she managed to whisper, "Yes."

"Touch it for me."

Josie cradled the phone against her ear and stroked her forefinger across her now-aroused clit. Her pussy grew warm beneath her touch. She moved her finger in small circles that soon had her biting her lip to hold back a moan.

"Open up the front of your blouse. Your tits must look so fine in that bra. I wish I were there to suck your nipples."

She wished the same thing. With her free hand, Josie did as Jack had told her. Her flesh was creamy white against the black lace. Her nipples pushed at the front, and she ran her palm over one before tweaking it between her thumb and finger. Her pussy was slick with her arousal, and she slid a finger down to bring some of her moisture up to her clit.

Another crackle of static reminded her where Jack was. "Don't wreck."

He chuckled. "I pulled over. I'm in a parking lot. I've got my prick in my hand right now, Josie, wishing it were in your mouth."

A mental image filled her head. Jack, his tie loosened and his suit pants undone, his thick, long cock gripped firmly in his fist. He wouldn't be wearing his earrings on the job, but his eyes would be shaded by mirrored sunglasses. She pictured the way his tongue would snake across his full mouth as he concentrated on pleasuring himself. In her mind, his strokes grew faster, and so did hers.

Her fingers danced on her bud, stroking and pinching. "I'm going to come."

His groan sent her toward the edge even faster. "Me, too. Talk to me, Josie. What are you thinking about?"

"I'm thinking about you kneeling here in front of me," she whispered, even in her arousal aware she was still at work. "You put your face between my legs, and you lick my pussy until I come."

Jack gave a wordless groan she recognized. "And then what?"

"And then you'd fill me up with your cock and fuck me."

As she said the words, her body shook with climax. His muffled cry told her he'd come, too. Josie pressed her palm to her beating clit as the shudders wracked her. At last, she was still. She pulled her skirt back down and put her feet on the floor. "Jack?"

"I'm here." She heard the smile in his voice. "Oh, shit. I'm going to be late. I'll see you tonight. I love you."

The words never failed to move her. "Love you, too. See you later."

He disconnected, and she hung up the phone. There was something to be said about middle-of-the-day sex, she mused as she bent back to tackle her To Do list. It made going to work a whole lot more fun.

THREE

"Are you planning on moving back home for good or just going for a few days?" Jack watched Josie carrying the last load toward his car.

She looked down at what she had in her arms. "I need my body pillow and my bed pillow. Sleeping on the futon is not going to be fun."

He waggled his eyebrows at her. "I'll make it fun."

"Don't be so sure," she replied. "You know Mom will have the old army cot set up for you."

Jack took the bag she'd slung over her shoulder and shoved it into the trunk. "You didn't tell her yet, did you?"

"I tried to. But you know my mom. It's hard to get a word in edgewise." Josie stuffed her pillows on top of the suitcases and closed the trunk, then turned to face him sternly. "Did you tell your parents?"

Jack made a show of looking at his watchless wrist. "Oh, man. Look at the time. We'd better get on the road. Traffic is going to be nuts."

"Jack." Josie reached for his arm. "Maybe we don't need to tell them for a while."

He linked his fingers through hers. "Why don't you want to tell them?"

"I don't know." She sighed. "I guess I just want this to be ours for a while longer. Just ours. I don't want to share it with anyone."

He nodded and pulled her close for a hug. "We share it with our downstairs neighbors about five times a week and twice on Sundays, Josie."

Their downstairs neighbor, a cranky Goth artist who insisted on being called Mina in homage to Bram Stoker's heroine, had taken to pounding on her ceiling whenever they made the least bit of noise. They'd been making quite a bit of noise since they'd moved in.

Josie sighed. "Once we share it with family, though, it'll get too big."

"I didn't think it could be too big."

"Jack, I'm serious."

He squeezed her. "I know you are, baby."

She tilted her head to look up at him. "They'll start making insinuations about getting married, having kids. All that stuff."

He got a funny look on his face. "And?"

She shrugged. "I'm not ready for all that speculation."

"We've been together for seven months. You're going to have to tell them some time."

"Oh, listen to you," she countered. "You haven't told your folks either!"

He grinned without shame. "You're right."

She looked at the car, filled with their luggage. "If we tell them now, they won't let us sleep together, you know."

"Then we won't tell them!" Jack's protest made her laugh. "Not until it's time to go home. Okay?"

"Okay. Let's go."

She was silent on the drive. Thinking. There was really no reason not to tell her family she and Jack were now a couple. She looked over at him, his fingers tapping on the steering wheel along with the music from the radio. Her love for him made anything she'd ever felt for any other man seem like a schoolgirl crush. She couldn't imagine the rest of her life without him.

And still, she wanted to keep him to herself for a while longer. It was selfish. She knew that, but as soon as they told their families, the speculation would start. When were they going to get married? Settle down? Have kids?

For now, Josie only wanted to ride what they had, enjoy it. Love Jack without thinking too hard about the future.

"Penny for your thoughts," Jack said. "Fifty cents to act them out."

"I'm worth more than fifty cents," she replied archly.

"Baby, you worth at least a buck-fitty."

She laughed. "Gee, thanks."

"Seriously, Josie. What are you so quiet about?"

"You want to know a reason why I love you so much?" she said. "Because you'd even bother to ask."

He reached for her hand. "Why wouldn't I?"

"Believe me, Jack. There are plenty of guys who wouldn't give a damn what their girlfriend was thinking about."

"Girlfriend." He snorted.

She looked at him. "What's funny about that?"

"It just sounds funny. Girlfriend. Like we're in junior high. Will you be my girlfriend? Yes, no, maybe. Circle one."

"Well, whatever you want to call me, most guys wouldn't care what I was thinking about."

They rode in silence for a moment more. Then he said, "Lover."

"What?"

"Lover. That's what I'd call you. Or my woman."

She had to look at him hard to see if he was being silly. "Your *woman*?"

He shot her a glance as he eased into the line of traffic entering the Pennsylvania Turnpike. "Yeah. My wo-man."

Josie rolled her eyes, but was secretly pleased in a strange way. "Wo-man, huh?"

"Yeah, because when I see you, I say, 'Whoa, man!'"

"Jack!" She began to laugh. "You are too much."

He took her hand and put it near his crotch. "Never too much for you, baby."

Just like that, she was wet for him. All it took was a simple cocky grin, a suggestive phrase, and she was imagining taking him in her mouth. A moan slipped from her mouth before she could catch it.

He glanced at her again. "Josie?"

She rubbed her fingers on the soft, worn denim of his jeans and was rewarded with a hardening bulge. "Watch the road."

She unbuckled her seatbelt and slid across the seat toward him. His zipper stuck but she tugged, then folded open his jeans. As usual, he wore dark boxer briefs. His erection pushed at the front, and she slid him free. He pulsed in her hand. She leaned over and took him into her mouth.

He muttered a curse that had her smiling around his cock. She sucked lightly on the tip, then slid her mouth down as far as she could. The position was awkward and she couldn't get him too far into her mouth without his zipper branding her cheek, so she concentrated on the head.

A slippery jewel of pre-come glimmered, and she used her finger to rub it into his skin.

He shifted to allow her better access. His hand cupped the back of her head. She took him deeper, then withdrew to roll her tongue around his cock head. He groaned, and she lifted her head to remind him, "Watch the road!"

"I'm watching, I'm watching. Don't worry, I won't do a Parenthood."

She remembered the scene from the Steve Martin flick, when the couple crashed their van because the wife was giving the husband a blow job. "I sure hope not."

She bent back to her task. Josie had never minded oral sex, not like some of her female friends who moaned and groaned about the effort it took to give a good blow job. Josie figured if she was going to let a man go down on her, she should at least consider returning the favor.

But sucking Jack wasn't about returning favors. She did it for the pure and simple pleasure of it. She loved making love to him, loved giving him pleasure. She got off just knowing what she was doing was going to make him come.

The soothing noise of the engine helped her find the rhythm. She clenched her thighs together, a trick she'd mastered a long time ago to get herself off when touching herself wasn't an option. It took a while, and it didn't always work, but she thought right now it might.

The car rocked along the smooth pavement. Josie's clit rubbed at the front of her panties with each squeeze of her thighs. She loved Jack with her mouth, and as the first bright sparks of orgasm began to tingle in her pussy, she felt him convulse under her tongue.

She took him as deep as she could. His hand tightened on her head. She took everything he had as her body twitched with climax. She held him in her mouth for a moment, until he let go of her hair, and then she tucked him back inside his jeans and sat back in her seat.

"That was nice." Jack ran a hand over his head.

Josie smiled and reached across to squeeze his shoulder. "Just say whoa."

FOUR

By the time Jack pulled into the driveway, shadows had begun to pool beneath the huge trees lining the street. Inside the large, three-story house, golden pools of light filled the windows. Josie could see people moving inside.

"Looks like we're the last ones here."

Jack pocketed the keys.

"Are you ready?" Josie gave him a grin.

Jack pretended to shudder. "I think so."

She squeezed his hand. "Let's go!"

The minute they stepped through the front door, they were descended upon.

"Aunt Josie! Uncle Jack!" five small voices cried, and her nieces and nephews flung themselves at her knees.

Jack scooped up the smallest child, two-year-old Sam, and swung the little boy into the air. "Hey, Sammy!"

Sam's dark brown eyes crinkled with joy as he giggled, and the other kids began clamoring for their turn.

"Me, too!"

"Swing me Uncle Jack!"

"Me, too! Me, too!"

He was so good with kids. For a startling moment, Josie pictured Jack cradling an infant. Their child. She met his eyes across the top of Sam's curly dark head, and time seemed to stop for a minute as she thought about what it would be like to have a baby with Jack.

Then the hall exploded into a cacophony of hugging, kissing and greeting. Francine Gold plastered smooches all over Josie's face before turning to Jack and pulling him down to leave pink lipstick prints all over his cheeks.

"What's with the baldy still?" She rubbed the cropped scruff of his hair. "You have such lovely hair, Jack."

"Yeah, for a Brillo pad," he said.

Francine tutted. "Oh, hush. It's good to see you."

Jack's father came and slapped Jack heartily on the shoulder and shook his hand before embracing Josie. "How's my girl?"

"I'm great, Ben." Josie gave the older man an affectionate squeeze. "It's good to see you."

Ava swooped into the hall, wiping her hands on her apron. Flour dusted one cheek, and her glasses were askew. "You made it!"

Josie father Dan peeked around the corner of the dining room doorway. "Does this mean we can finally eat?"

"Hi, Dad." Josie wove her way through the crowd to give him a kiss. "Sorry we're late. Traffic."

Her dad jerked his head toward the table glittering with china and silverware. "We were afraid we'd have to start without you."

Ava flapped her apron at her husband. "As if we could start without Josie and Jack!"

The other relatives and Josie's siblings began to filter into the dining room from the rest of the house. There were more kisses and hugs, more exclamations, but at last they all seated themselves at the table. Josie got up to help her mom and the other women serve.

"Holy cow, Mom. Will you have anything left for tomorrow night's Seder?" Josie looked around the kitchen. Every inch of counter and table space was covered with plates and containers of food.

"You know your mom," said her sister-in-law Rachael. "She's always afraid she won't have enough for everyone to eat."

Ava gave her daughter-in-law a glance. "Do I hear you complaining?"

Rachael laughed and gave Ava a hug around the shoulders. "Absolutely not. Any meal I don't have to cook is my favorite."

Her parents had invited many more people for tomorrow night's Seder, but tonight dinner was just for family. Josie looked around the table at the faces of the people she loved best, and her heart swelled with emotion. She looked down to the end of the table, where Jack sat in deep conversation with her brother Seth. The Golds had been part of their family for so long. Josie wondered how she could ever have thought she'd end up with someone else.

They ate, they drank, they laughed at stories and jokes. Children grew tired and were packed off to bath and bed, and still the food kept coming. At last, Josie pushed away from table with a sigh.

"No more!" she cried. "I won't be able to eat for a week!"

"Don't scare your mother like that," her dad said.

Josie got up and stretched. "I don't know about anybody else, but I need to go for a walk. I'll help with the dishes when I get back, Mom."

Ava grinned. "Not to worry, doll. I hired help this year."

That surprised her. "You did?"

Ava shrugged. "After all these years of your dad telling me I should get some help so I could spend time with the family instead of getting dishpan hands, I took him up on it. You remember Avery Compton, don't you?"

"From next door?" Josie recalled a tiny girl with blonde pigtails and permanently scraped knees.

"She's home for spring break from college and she's bringing a friend to come over and clean up."

Josie mentally staggered. "College? Wow."

"See?" Ava said with a significant look and a wag of her finger. "Time flies. None of us are getting any younger."

"Walk time," Josie replied, not wanting to listen to another lecture from her mom about when she was going to settle down.

"I'll go with you," Jack said. "I need some exercise, too."

"You watch out for Josie," Francine said. "It's dark out there and dangerous for a young woman walking alone."

Once again, Josie locked eyes with Jack. His mouth quirked into a grin that turned her insides into liquid heat.

"I'll take care of her, Mom. I always do."

What was it about sexual innuendo that made it sexier when it was forbidden? Josie didn't know, but the hidden meaning in his words had her breath catch in her throat.

Together they went out the front door and down the sidewalk. The April air was still cool at night, though the days had started to warm considerably. Josie paused to peer down at the dirt along the walk.

"Everything's starting to bloom."

Jack took her hand. "It will be summer before we know it."

"You're not going to start, too, are you?" Josie giggled. "What's this fetish with time you and my mom have?"

"I have a fetish," Jack replied. "But it has nothing to do with time."

That sounded promising. "Oh, really?"

He swung their linked hands. "Oh, no, baby. It's all about dogging."

She might have expected a lot of things, but not that. "What on earth is that?"

"Dogging is having sex in public places," Jack explained so matter-of-factly he might have been discussing how to buy stocks. "In cars or whatever. And sometimes, people watch and join in."

"Ew, Jack! That's nasty!"

In the darkness, she couldn't see his face to figure out if he was joking or not. When they entered the next pool of light from the overhead streetlamp, she stopped and pulled him around to get a good look at his face.

"Are you serious?"

"About sex in a public place?" He gave her one of his patented thigh-spreading grins. "Hell, yeah."

She put her hands on her hips. "About people watching."

"Hey, Josie, I can't help it if people catch a glimpse. That's the risk you take when you're doing it in public."

"How many times have you done this?" she asked suspiciously, and a trifle jealously.

"Dogging?" He paused, making her sweat. "Never. I saw it on the internet."

"I'm not even going to ask how you got on that website." She looked around. They'd walked down the hill from her parents' house and were in front of an old elementary school. In the dark, the playground equipment looked like excavated dinosaur bones.

"How about sex in public?" she whispered.

He pulled her into his arms. "Well, now, I can't say that I've ever actually done that either."

Josie took him by the hand and led him down the concrete path toward the playground. When they left the path, the grass whispered against their feet until they reached the thick covering of wood shavings beneath the swing set.

"I think you're going to get lucky," she told him.

Josie chose the largest swing and settled Jack into it. This part of the playground was not only nearly pitch black, but also secluded behind the other equipment. Not even anyone walking by on the sidewalk would be able to see them. Still, the knowledge they were out in public added to the thrill of unsnapping his jeans and unzipping his zipper.

Josie lifted her skirt and slid her panties down, then tucked them into her pocket for safekeeping. The chilly air made gooseflesh break out on her legs and arms, but she was hot between her legs.

"Josie, you're a dirty, dirty girl."

"And you love it."

She caught the flash of his teeth in the darkness as he grinned. "I sure do."

Now came the tricky part. As kids, they'd ridden double on these very swings, one person on the seat and the other facing him on his lap. The question was, would they still be able to do it that way?

She grabbed hold of the swing's chain with one hand and slid her leg around Jack's waist. Jack's hands gripped and lifted her ass, helping her as she held herself up on the chain to slide her other leg around. For a moment she hovered, hands clenching the chains, and then she found his cock with her slick pussy and lowered herself onto Jack's lap.

She wiggled a little until he slid inside her all the way, then let go of the chains and put her hands on his shoulders. Jack still had his hands under her ass. His feet were planted solidly on the ground while she crossed her ankles behind his back. She was suspended, impaled on his prick.

His mouth found hers. His tongue dove deep inside, stroking her. He put the swing in motion, slowly but steadily. Every movement back and forth rocked her clit against his firm belly and thrust his cock deeper inside her.

His teeth nibbled at hers lips, then found her ear and the soft flesh of her neck and throat. "Hang on."

She gripped him more tightly with her arms and legs. Jack slid his hands out from under her and held onto the chains. Then he really began to swing.

He pushed off from the ground, lifted his muscular legs and tilted his body back. Josie let out a muffled squeal and clung to him. For a moment, the sensation was so unsettling she forgot to concentrate on the pleasure. Jack wouldn't let her fall. The thought calmed her and she relaxed enough to focus again on the way his stomach rubbed her clit back and forth with every swing.

In this position, he couldn't slide in and out as far as he would normally, but the swing did all the work for them. They swung back and Jack's knees curled to push his feet off the ground. Forward and he straightened his legs to get them airborne. Pumping the swing as he was pumping her.

They weren't swinging terribly high; they'd certainly gone higher and faster when they were kids. It was high enough. They were flying, together. Weightless.

The air rushed past her face and cooled her heated

cheeks. Her fingers began to ache from hanging on to the chain. Her thighs burned from the chain cutting into her flesh. She'd be lucky if she could stand when this was done, but Josie couldn't, at that moment, care.

His pumps became staggered, less smooth. His breath panted in her ear. He breathed her name.

She needed just little more pressure. A few more pumps. Just...a little more....

She began to quiver at the same time she felt him throb inside her. He let go of the swing with one hand and used it to clasp her to him, tight, and he bit down on the curve of her shoulder.

Her neck hurt, her hands hurt, her thighs hurt, but the ecstasy thrumming through her canceled out the pain. If anything, the myriad of small hurts made the pleasure even sweeter.

Slowly, the swing stopped. Jack hugged her and nuzzled the spot he'd bitten. She let go of the chains and put her arms around his shoulders again.

"I can't move," she said after a minute.

Jack's deep, rumbling chuckle tickled her ears. "My ass feels like it's on fire. And I don't mean that in a good way."

"Seriously, Jack. I can't move."

"Not a problem." Jack got to his feet and supported her weight on his hands until she could unwrap her legs from around his waist.

Her skirt fell around her ankles and she plucked her panties from her pocket and slipped them back on. "You okay?"

She loved the way he was always so concerned about her. "Great. You?"

She heard the zip and snap of his pants. "Never better."

"We'd better get back."

She found herself engulfed in his embrace. She leaned against his broad chest and drank in the scent of him. His arms were warm. She rubbed her cheek against the softness of his shirt and gave a huge, contented sigh. Jack smoothed his hand over her back, then squeezed.

They didn't say anything, but then, they didn't have to.

FIVE

Josie woke up with a crick in her neck and an aching back, despite the pillows she'd surrounded herself with. The windowless family room was still black, but the thumps and thuds overhead told her morning had arrived. Jack's soft snuffles kept her from dozing off again. At home, she'd have elbowed him to turn over, but with him stretched out on the army cot a few feet away, all she could do was lob a pillow at him and hope it struck.

In another minute it didn't matter because the bright overhead lights came on and five pairs of small feet thundered down the stairs. Josie had just enough time to shield her eyes from the glare before her nieces and nephews hurtled into the room and onto the futon. It creaked alarmingly under their combined, wriggling weight.

"Kids, don't damage Aunt Josie." Mim had followed the kids. "Good, you're up."

Jack had buried his head beneath his pillow, and his reply was muffled. "We are now!"

Josie curled up with Max on her left and Sam on her

right. The girls, Hannah, Sarah and Rebecca, bounced up and down and giggled. "Morning."

"I tried to keep them upstairs as long as I could," her sister Miriam said. "But they were dying to get down to see you."

"No problem." Josie snuggled with her nephews for another moment before tumbling them off her in a fit of giggles. She got up and stretched out the soreness in her back.

"What'd you do to your hands?" Mim sounded concerned, and Josie looked at the scrape marks the chains had made last night.

"Nothing," she said vaguely. "Hey, Mim, how about we take the kids to the zoo today?"

"We?"

"Me and Jack."

Jack stuck his head out from under the pillow. "What are you volunteering me for?"

"The zoo." Josie bent to push Sarah's tangled hair out of her face.

Jack yawned and sat up, scrubbing his face. "Do I have a choice?"

"Nope." Josie staggered under the weight of her nephews and nieces clambering on top of her, shouting. "Unless you want to stay here and make matzo balls."

"Zoo it is." Jack got up and rolled his neck on his shoulders, then cracked his back. "Lemme grab a shower."

He left the room to use the small bathroom. Mim's eyes followed him as she shooed the kids toward the family room's couch and television. When they'd been settled in front of some inane cartoon adventure Josie didn't recognize, her sister turned to her.

"What on earth is wrong with you?"

Josie had been fumbling in her suitcase for a toothbrush and shampoo. Her sister's question made her look up, confused. "What do you mean?"

"I mean that guy has a body on him that could make a nun horny. I mean what's wrong with you that you haven't snapped him off the market already?"

Josie bit back a smile. "Mim, that's none of your business."

Mim rolled her eyes and gave Josie the big-sister death look. "Don't tell me you have somebody else."

"Actually, no."

"Then what's up?"

Josie shook her head. "Fine, fine. Have it your way. The truth is, Jack and I have been humping like bunnies since September. We mostly do it twice a day, although sometimes we take a day off. My hands are scraped up, in fact, because last night on our walk we stopped and had mind-blowing sex on a swing at the playground."

Mim frowned. "Yeah, right. On a swing? You expect me to believe that?"

Josie shrugged. "It's true."

"Okay, fine." Mim threw up her hands in a gesture so like their mother's Josie had to grin. "Tell all kinds of stories. I'm just telling you, you have a prime catch right under your nose and you don't seem to be aware of it."

"Believe me, Mim," Josie said solemnly. "I'm totally aware."

Mim gave a snort of total disbelief. "A swing. Where'd you read about that, Playgirl magazine?"

"Mommy, what's Playgirl magazine?" Hannah asked.

"Never mind." Mim shot Josie a look. "C'mon, precious. Let's go get ready to go to the zoo."

Josie stared after her sister for a moment, then just

shook her head. Apparently, sometimes truth really was stranger than fiction. Then she went in search of a shower.

SIX

The day at the zoo passed quickly enough. Josie and Jack were heroes to her frazzled siblings, who'd welcomed the break from their spawn, and heroes to the kids, who'd run their aunt and "uncle" ragged. When they finally brought the children in the house, little Sam snuggled asleep on Jack's shoulder, everything had already been prepared for the first Seder.

The house had been full yesterday, but with more friends and family invited for the special Passover dinner, it was now bursting. Three leaves had been put into the table that had been Ava's grandmother's. A folding table, made fancy with a white cloth and drapes over the chairs had been set up for the overflow, and the kids had their own small table off to the side.

Everything gleamed and glittered. Flowers gave the tables a festive air. Josie breathed in the delicious scents of good home cooking—matzo ball soup, roast turkey, brisket.

"Time to get started, everyone!" Dan Levine's booming voice got everyone moving to find their place cards, charmingly scrawled in Hannah's childish hand.

This time, Jack and Josie's places were next to each other. The table was crowded, with chairs so close, once they sat down, it was almost impossible to get back up without moving the person on either side. Josie didn't mind. She was sitting on the end next to the wall. Jack, on the other hand, was between her and Mrs. Bergdorf, who smelled like mothballs.

When everyone had squeezed into their places, Dan began the Seder. Wine flowed as the participants followed the custom of consuming a minimum of four cups of wine. By the time it was time to eat dinner, Josie had a nice, tipsy buzz.

She was leaning her head against the wall, just enjoying the bustle and conversation, when Jack's elbow knocked his fork onto the floor at her feet.

"I'll get it," he said casually, and disappeared under the tablecloth hiding her lap.

He was only down there long enough to pick up the fork, but on his way back up he managed to slid her skirt up over her thighs and plant a kiss on the exposed flesh just above her knee.

He reappeared above the table, fork in hand, his face as neutral as though he'd done nothing untoward. Josie's cheeks had heated.

"More wine, Josephine?" Aunt Bea asked. "You look flushed. Are you all right?"

"Fine," Josie managed to croak.

She nudged Jack under the table. With his head still turned away from her, his hand swiveled around and caressed her thigh. Beneath the cover of the long tablecloth, nobody would possibly have any idea what he was doing. But Josie did.

Dinner continued with more songs and prayers, but for

once, Josie barely joined in. Jack's hand on her was too distracting. He wasn't touching her anyplace too naughty, but he was close enough to make her think about him touching her there, and the thought was enough to make her slick with arousal.

At last, dinner was over, dessert consumed, and the door had been opened for Elijah. Seth, who'd snuck out during dessert, appeared in the doorway clothed in biblical garb and a white wig and beard, and gave special Passover chocolates to the kids. The adults drank a final glass of wine, the children found the hidden piece of matzo and earned their gifts, and the Seder was finished.

Josie and Jack were among the last to leave the table, since they'd been seated so far to the back. The entire time her family and friends got up and made their various ways home, to the living room for coffee, or to bed, Josie sat and felt Jack's hand on her thigh.

When at last they, too, could leave the table, her legs were shaky and her pulse pounding. She'd have sworn his fingers had left a permanent imprint on her skin.

She was so aroused she thought all he'd need to do was kiss her, and she'd splinter into climax. There'd be no kissing of that nature right now, of course. She felt awful even imagining it, what with Aunt Flo regaling them with stories about her dogs and Uncle Marty telling knock-knock jokes.

Somehow, Josie made it through the rest of the evening. Everything had become super bright, super clear. She sat next to Jack on the living room sofa, her entire side alight with the sensation of his body pressing against hers. She talked, she laughed, she responded...but all she was thinking about was getting Jack naked.

What Jack was thinking about, she couldn't tell. He

reached casually across her to grab a handful of carrots from the veggie tray, and his arm "accidentally" brushed her breasts. He nudged her with his thigh. He every so often stretched out his arms and ran a surreptitious finger along the back of her neck, right where he knew she loved it the most. In short, he was being devilishly seductive. On purpose. She wanted to slap him, but she wanted to make love to him more. She'd slap him after.

Finally, everyone who wasn't sleeping over went home. Everyone else went to bed. They were left alone.

"My back is killing me," Jack said so nonchalantly she knew he had something up his sleeve. "I was thinking about going in the hot tub. Want to come?"

Boy, did she. Josie narrowed her eyes at him, but couldn't come right out and accuse him of doing his best to seduce her the entire night. Not when she didn't really mind.

"Sure," she said instead, in case anyone happened to be listening. "Sounds great."

Her parents had installed the five-person spa unit a few summers before. It had been a big hit with kids and older folks, but Jack and Josie had it to themselves tonight. The open roof of the gazebo allowed them to see the stars, while the latticed sides provided a privacy Josie knew they were going to need. They changed quickly and she followed Jack outside and watched his ass, clad only in a pair of black, form-fitting trunks, in appreciation.

He paused on the stairs to the tub and wiggled his butt for her. "Like what you see?"

"I like it better without the bathing suit."

"That can be arranged." He threw a wicked grin over his shoulder, then slipped his suit down over his thighs and hung it neatly on the hooks along the gazebo wall. "That better?"

"You're so bad."

"I know," he replied without a hint of guilt.

Josie watched him sink into the steaming water, then pulled off her own simple once-piece bathing suit and climbed into the water. It was almost too hot at first, but as soon as her body adjusted, she let out a long, contented sigh. The jets pounded her back in all the right places. The futon in the family room was large enough, just not very comfortable.

"Bliss," she murmured. "Pure bliss."

Jack slid over next to her and pulled her close. "Better than this?"

He kissed her, slowly and thoroughly, and when he was done, Josie was hotter than the water. "Nothing's better than that."

He kissed her again. She became aware that his hand had moved from her hip to the juncture of her thighs, and she spread her legs for him. He didn't touch her, not right away, but the swirling water did. It licked and stroked at her like a nimble tongue. She'd been aroused all night, and needed little extra stimulation to get even closer.

Jack cupped her breast, then rolled the nipple softly between his fingers. He gave it a gentle tweak that had her gasping against his mouth, and he chuckled. "You're so hot."

"Because of you." She pulled his mouth back to hers. Her tongue slid between his lips, and she took charge of the kiss.

His head tilted back. Josie let the water lift her as she slid onto his lap. Her pussy pressed against his stomach. The length of his erection slid between the crease of her buttocks to the bottom of her back. She rocked forward, pressing herself against him. He cupped her ass and held her close, then lifted her a little to bring his cock between them. Now his prick nestled against her clit and along her open folds. His hands moved her back and forth and up down in the water. Her clit rubbed on him, and in moments her slickness coated him.

He moved to position himself inside her, but Josie stopped him. She smiled at the questioning look in his eyes, then moved off his lap. She floated to the other side of the tub and knelt on the built-in seat. The curved plastic dipped low enough that she could lean forward and rest her elbows on the tub's side while the rest of her body stayed underwater. She looked over her shoulder and wiggled her ass at him.

"C'mon."

He did with a speed that amused her. He gripped her hips and put one knee next to hers on the seat, then pushed his cock inside her. The water rushed over them, caressing them. Her breasts tingled from the extra sensations. She shifted a little, tilted her pelvis just a touch, then reached down and fiddled with the directional jet.

The water shot out and rushed past her already engorged clit. The force of it made her give a low cry. She gripped the tub's sides with both hands while her heart and clit both pounded at the extra stimulation. Jack echoed her cry and bent low over her back. The water bubbled all around them.

He stopped moving for a moment. His hands tightened on her hips. The water rocked them so he barely had to thrust. Her clitoris throbbed at the tickling, teasing touch of the water jetting between her legs. When he began to move again, her first orgasm arced through her like sparks from a shorted wire. Another built almost immediately from the water jet's stimulation. Jack's thrusts moved her body, kept her clit from being directly in the spray, teased her, and still she cascaded into another frenzy of erotic sensation.

Jack surprised her when he stopped again. "I have to get out, Josie. It's too hot in here."

She nodded, not quite able to speak. Jack slid out of her, then got out of the tub altogether. She got out, too, grateful for the cool night air sliding across her sensitized body. She looked around the concrete slab, the splintery gazebo walls. "What now?"

Jack took the towel he'd brought out and spread it on the concrete. Then he lay on his back. Josie straddled him. He slid in as effortlessly as he had before. She waited a moment before beginning to move.

"I hope nobody decides to come out for a midnight soak."

Jack grinned up at her. Even in the dim light, she could see his normally tawny cheeks were flushed. "They'll get quite a surprise."

The urgency had worn off a bit, especially since she'd had two orgasms already. Josie was discovering she liked making love to Jack this way, with her pleasure taken care of. She began to roll her hips, then leaned forward to kiss him while she moved on him. His hands caressed her back, her shoulders, her hips and rear. He guided her pace, but didn't force her. They moved as one, in tune, in sync, perfectly.

She stopped kissing him so she could look into his dark eyes. He'd begun to bite his lower lip, a sign she knew. He was going to come soon. She could have tried for a third orgasm, forced her body to another burst of ecstasy, but she didn't bother. She was fulfilled. It was time for her to concentrate on Jack.

She slowed the pace and varied her thrusts. She lifted herself nearly all the way off his cock, then slid down, slowly, and twisted her hips. She pushed back on her heels and used her feet to lift her up and down while she steadied herself with her hands on his chest. She pinched his flat, taut nipples, one after the other, in time with the pace of her lovemaking.

His breath caught in his chest. His hips lifted off the ground, moving her. Josie clenched her inner muscles as she slid up and down. Twisting her back, she reached around between Jack's legs and let her fingers trail along the soft sac of his balls. They tightened beneath her touch. His cock throbbed within her.

She bent back to him again and caught his last strangled cry in her mouth as she kissed him. His final thrust pushed her against him so fiercely their teeth crashed together. Pain flared in her lip and she let out a muffled "Ouch!"

"You bit me," Josie said. She held up her fingers, which were spotted with red from where she'd touched her lip. She began to laugh. "Geez, Jack."

He wiped the small drops of blood from her lip and pulled her down to kiss him again. "Sorry, baby. You got me carried away."

When he got to his feet, she saw one elbow was scraped raw from contact with the rough cement. "We're the walking wounded!"

"Hazards of the sport," Jack said. "Next time I'm going to wear my protective gear."

"You're a goofball." Josie stood on her tiptoes to kiss him. "But I love you anyway."

Jack smoothed her wet hair off her forehead. "Do you, Josie?"

"Of course I do." She tilted her head to look at him. "What's wrong?"

"Nothing." He smiled, not his usual cocky grin, but a softer curving of his lips. "Just making sure."

She looped her arms around his waist and put her head on his chest, content to feel the beat of his heart on her cheek. "How could I not, after all this time?"

He squeezed her. She felt the point of his chin rest on top of her head. "Sometimes I feel like this is just a dream, and when I wake up, we'll be back to playing The Game."

She thought of the contest they used to share, to see who could win the most points by getting members of the opposite sex to flirt with them. "This isn't The Game."

"Good thing," Jack said. "'Cause I totally just scored."

Josie waited until he'd turned to step back into his swimming trunks before she locker-room towel-snapped him.

SEVEN

"Bring up the folding chairs," Ava ordered Seth. She turned to Mim. "Grab the extra tablecloth from the cabinet. We'll put the second folding table over here."

Josie grinned as Mim made a face behind their mother's back. "Mom, how many people did you invite?"

Ava shook her head. "Don't ask."

Jack peeked in the doorway. "Ava, where do you want this sliced turkey?"

Ava gave orders and the house bustled. In the whirlwind of activity, Josie had little time to spend with Jack. He cornered her in the den and stole a kiss, but that was the extent of their contact.

"What's going on with you?" Mim asked suspiciously as she and Josie peeled mounds of potatoes for dinner.

Ava, fully convinced the Y-chromosome was incompatible with culinary skill, had chased all the men outside to play flag football with the kids. Josie looked out the kitchen window as Jack allowed her nieces and nephews to tackle him to the ground. She couldn't help smiling.

"What do you mean?" she asked her sister.

"You and Jack. You barely speak to him. You won't look him in the eye. You guys have been friends too long, Josie. I remember when he used to come over here with his Superman cape and you'd be Wonder Woman. Did you have a fight?"

"No." Josie dumped her potato peelings into the garbage and looked up at her sister. "Mim, you know sometimes relationships change."

Mim's brow furrowed. "Yes."

"And Jack and I have been friends forever. But we're not kids anymore. We're grownups."

Now Mim put down her paring knife and gave her younger sister a hard stare. "Yes."

Josie wanted to tell her sister. She really did. She wanted to giggle over her relationship with Jack like they'd used to do when they were in high school, talking about their crushes. Mim would be happy for her, and yet, Josie hesitated.

She watched as Jack bent to show little Sam how to throw the football, and tenderness filled her. Surprising tears filled her eyes at the depth of her feelings. She swiped at her eyes, embarrassed to be acting so corny.

"Jojo, what's wrong?" Mim sounded concerned. "Why are you crying?"

Josie laughed. "Oh, Mim. I'm not. It's just that—"

Mim frowned and took Josie's hand. "Whatever it is, you can tell me. Are you pregnant?"

"What?" Josie spluttered. "No!"

"Sick?"

"No, Mim. Listen—"

Mim sighed. "So it is a problem with Jack."

"It's not a problem, Mim." Again, Josie opened her mouth to tell her sister that she and Jack were lovers. Before she could, the back door swung open and the troops tramped into the kitchen, declaring they were starving and needed food.

Ava, who'd been busy arranging the tables and chairs to accommodate all the extra people she'd invited, swooped in to prepare lunch and direct traffic. The chaos swirled around Josie, and she sighed. Her news would have to wait for another time.

She caught sight of Jack, his dark eyes twinkling as he snatched a leftover piece of roast beef from Ava's platter. He caught Josie's eye, and they shared a smile before Ava distracted him with a scolding.

With so much going on, Mim didn't have time to cross-examine Josie again. The day passed too quickly, especially when guests started arriving in the late afternoon for what her mother called a pre-Seder nosh.

"I don't think I've ever seen so much food in my entire life." Jack nodded toward the living room, where the coffee and end tables had been loaded with trays of snacks.

"Sure you have. At your mother's house," Josie countered. She stepped out of the way as the children, who seemed to have multiplied, thundered through the house.

"Oh, yeah." Jack grinned. "Want something to eat?"

Josie put a hand to her belly. "I'm saving myself for dinner."

"I'll be glad to help you with dessert." Jack bent low to whisper in her ear.

Josie's entire body hummed at the sensation of his lips brushing her ear. She nudged him with her elbow. "I'll bet."

He chuckled and nuzzled her neck. Everything else in the house, in the world, faded away. Josie leaned against his broad chest and drank in his scent with her eyes closed.

When she opened them, he had stopped smiling and stared at her seriously.

"What?" she asked.

He pushed a tendril of hair away from her eyes. "I just like looking at you."

"Aunt Josie?"

She looked down to the small boy at her leg. "Hi, Sammy."

He held up an action figure that had lost a leg. "Fix?"

"Sure, honey." She fiddled with the broken toy, then handed it back. "All better?"

Her nephew nodded then lifted his arms in silent command. Jack picked him up. Sam showed Jack the toy.

"Aunt Josie fix."

"Your Aunt Josie is pretty amazing isn't she, Sam?"

Sam smiled. "Mazin'!"

"Do you want to know how much I love Aunt Josie?"

Sam's small face scrunched with thought. "How much?"

"To the moon and back, little guy." Jack's eyes caught hers again.

"Me too," Sam said, struggling to get down. He scampered off.

"Walk with me outside," Jack said quietly, just as Ava's voice reverberated throughout the house.

"Dinner time!"

"After dinner," he amended.

"It's a promise." Josie squeezed his hand, and they headed off for the dining room.

The second night's Seder was no less elaborate than the first. Ava and Dan had invited many of their friends and neighbors in addition to the family, and there wasn't an inch to spare at any of the tables. Josie watched her parents fondly as they led the group in the prayers and rituals that had been practiced for so many years. It was good to be a part of a family, especially one that loved and respected each other the way hers did. She knew many families who had constant strife. She was lucky.

She looked over at Jack's parents, already so much a part of her family. Francine nodded thoughtfully at something Jack was saying, and Ben amused the children with a magic trick. Jack favored his parents' easy manner and sense of humor. He was as much their son as he could have been had he been born to them instead of adopted. Francine had often remarked Josie was like the daughter she'd never been able to have. What would Jack's mother say about Jack and Josie being in love?

"Psst." Seth got Josie's attention. "Can you be Elijah tonight?"

Josie smiled at her brother. "Pressure too much for you?"

He returned the grin. "No, but I think Sam's on to me. He won't suspect you."

"Sure." While the rest of the horde was engaged in eating and talking, Josie excused herself quietly and went to the garage where the Elijah costume was kept.

As she pulled on the long brown robe, the garage door opened. Expecting to see one of the children, Josie turned, but it was Jack. "You scared me!"

"Sorry." He didn't sound sorry. "I saw you sneak away. I thought I'd come see what you were up to."

"Seth asked me to be Elijah. Help me get this wig on."

"You'd better hurry," Jack said. "They're going to open the door in about three minutes."

"Oops!" Giggling, Josie scrambled into the wig and beard, then ducked out through the door to the outside. She ran around the front walk toward the door they'd be opening as part of the Seder ritual.

She peeked in through the dining room windows and waited for her father to get up to open the door. Dan was still talking. She had a few minutes to spare.

"Josie, wait a minute. I want to talk to you."

She turned, not certain what to expect, but stunned to see the look on Jack's face. "What's wrong?"

He looked like he'd just seen a ghost. In the small golden squares of light spilling from the dining room windows, Jack's skin had a decidedly paler cast to it than normal. Josie stepped toward him.

"Jack?"

His eyes cut to the windows, where her dad was still talking. "I love you."

"I love you, too." Unease settled in the pit of her stomach. "Why do I feel a 'but' coming on?"

"No but." Now he gave her the grin she was used to, though it shone at half-wattage. He ran a hand over his head and bit at his lower lip. "Josie..."

She'd never seen him at such a loss for words. Josie pulled off the wig and beard and clutched them in her hand. She waited for him to speak.

"This isn't the right time." He looked back toward the house. "I'm an idiot, Josie. I'm sorry."

Nervousness made her snappish. "What the hell is going on, Jack? What's the matter? Oh, God." She swallowed. "You came out here to tell me you don't want to be with me any more, didn't you?"

"No!" Jack's voice was loud enough to be heard inside, if anyone was listening. "Of course not!"

"Then what?" Belligerently, Josie put her hands on her hips. "I hate when you do this to me, Jack!"

She'd put him on the defensive. "Do what?"

She waved her hands. "This! How you always manage to sneak in some heavy-duty news at the wrong time, so you don't have to tell me the truth right away! Like when you crashed my car, and you tried to tell me just before I was going in for that important job interview."

"That was one time."

She narrowed her eyes at him. "If you've got something to say to me, Jacob Gold, you'd better say it now, before that door opens and I become Elijah."

Jack took a deep breath. "I didn't want it to be like this."

"Jack," she began warningly.

He stunned her into utter silence when he went to one knee in front of her and took her hand. The dark velvet box in his hand made her mouth drop open. The breath hissed from her lungs.

"Josie, I love you. I've loved you for so long I can't even remember a time when I didn't. I don't want to imagine being without you." He cracked open the box to reveal the glittering diamond ring inside. "Will you marry me?"

The front door opened at that moment, spilling bright light and squawking children out on the stoop. The wig and beard fell from Josie's limp fingers as she put her hand over the one Jack held. From the corner of her eye she saw her family and friends pushing out onto the porch to welcome Elijah, and she had time to smile at the surprise they were going to have instead.

"Of course I will," she told Jack.

From the stoop she heard her mother murmur, "Look at the lovebirds."

Mim cried out, "I knew it!"

Francine began to sob with joy, or so Josie hoped, and

the children hooted and hollered for their candy. She ignored all of them.

The only thing that mattered was the man in front of her. The man she loved. Jack got to his feet and swept her into his arms. His kiss was the sweetest thing she'd ever known.

"The door's open," Jack whispered against her mouth, as though he'd only now just noticed.

"I know." She kissed him again. "Now all we have to do is walk through it."

As usual, she didn't have to explain what she meant. He already knew. Josie glanced toward the windows, where at least a dozen people were pretending not to watch.

"It's going to be interesting," she said with a sigh.

Jack looked at their audience. "Yeah. But we'll make it. Together."

Then he kissed her again, and Josie didn't bother to worry anymore.

WHITE WEDDING

ONE

"Hey, little sister. What have you done?"

Josie Levine made a face at her sister's awful Billy Idol impersonation. "Nice, Mim."

Mim grinned and pulled the veil off her head, then put it back on the rack. "It's not you. Too frou-frou."

Josie sighed, staring at her reflection in the boutique's full-length mirror. "Can we just go?"

Frowning, Mim turned. "Why? We just got here."

Josie gestured at the cascade of ruffles and lace adorning the pristine white gown. "You're right, Mim. This is so not me."

"I know." Mim fluffed one of the leg-o-mutton sleeves. "But there are others."

Josie sighed again. "I've tried on every dress in this shop. I'm just ready to go home."

Mim smiled and patted Josie's arm. "Want to go get some coffee?"

Thank heavens for older sisters who know just what to say, Josie thought as Mim nodded and gestured for the boutique attendant to come over and help Josie out of the dress.

All at once, Josie's throat had closed so tightly she could only nod.

At the coffee shop, firmly ensconced behind a plate of cheesecake and an extra large chocolate raspberry latte, Josie felt better. Or at least, no longer like she was going to burst into horrified tears at the sight of herself in a wedding gown.

Mim sipped her own drink and watched her sister before saying, "So, what's wrong?"

"Oh, Mim." Josie sighed. "Nothing. Everything."

"Is it Jack?"

Josie shook her head. "No. Jack's still Jack."

"You're having cold feet?"

It wasn't that...exactly. She and Jack been friends since childhood, lovers for just about a year, and if she was going to marry anyone, it would have to be Jack. She didn't mind the thought of being married. It was the *getting* married that had her sweating.

Mim smiled in sympathy. "Is Mom giving you a hard time? Remember, I've been through this already."

"Mom's been...fine." Josie smiled. "And Mrs. Gold's been...fine."

Mim laughed. "Mom and Mrs. Gold both planning a wedding. God help you, Josie, because nobody else can."

At least she could still laugh. For now. "Mim, if it's not one of them on the phone, it's the other. And the emails, oy!" She put her face in her hands. "Mrs. Gold even instant messages me!"

"No way!" Mim laughed, as though imagining Jack's mother at the computer. "What's her username?"

"Hopefulgranny1241." Josie rolled her eyes. "Like that's subtle."

"Sorry," Mim said, wiping her eyes. "I'm not trying to laugh at you. But..."

"Go ahead and laugh," Josie said. "If I can't laugh at it, I don't know what I'd do."

"You'll get through it," Mim promised and squeezed Josie's hand. "I did."

"I've got four more months," said Josie with a sigh.

"It will be over before you know it."

"I hope so." She wasn't sure she could survive much longer than that.

TWO

"To the left. Yes, right there." Josie groaned as Jack's fingers found the magic spot and began rubbing. "Mmm. That's so good."

He chuckled and kept rubbing. "Geez, Josie. You're so tense."

He stroked his fingers down the sides of her neck, then moved them back to the knots in her shoulders. Practically purring, she arched into his touch. "You've got magic fingers."

He rubbed harder, finding the knots and pushing them in the hurts-so-good way that made her squirm. "That better?"

Josie melted under his touch, her arms and legs growing limp under Jack's ministrations. She closed her eyes, feeling him move his hands up and down her back, then lower, to caress her butt briefly before moving back up to knead her shoulders again.

She grinned into the pillow, her eyes closed, but said nothing. The next time his hands slid down to pass over her ass, she lifted her hips a little bit and heard him chuckle low, under his breath. She kept her eyes closed, still smiling. A new tension coiled in her stomach, unrelated to the earlier tight muscles in her neck and shoulders. But just as easily soothed by Jack's hands.

He rubbed her shoulders, then walked his fingers down along the sides of her spine, making it crackle. He ended up at her rear again, each of his hands big enough to cup one of her cheeks. The heat of his palms warmed her skin through the cotton of her panties. Josie made a low noise in her throat, not quite a groan and not quite a moan. More like a whisper of assent. She pushed upward against his hands, and he slipped one beneath her, sliding under the waistband of her panties with ease and parting her curls with one finger.

With her eyes still closed, Josie's senses had heightened. The bed dipped as he stretched out next to her, pulling her onto her side to spoon against him, her back against his chest. They'd both stripped down to underwear before he'd begun the massage. His bare skin on hers made her press back against him.

His mouth found the back of her neck just below the hairline, in the exact place she loved him to kiss. His tongue's wet heat flicked along her skin, making her shiver, and the scrape of his teeth made her sigh. The finger between her legs kept up the steady, slow circling he knew drove her wild.

His cock nestled in the crack of her buttocks, separated by the thin layers of their underwear. Josie moved her hips, rocking in time with Jack's hand. He nibbled her neck and nuzzled the hollow of her shoulder as he continued to stroke her.

He dipped his finger along her folds, bringing some of her liquid heat up to slide along her clitoris. That extra bit of sensation, the smoothness, made her shiver. His lips curved on her skin and she heard the smile in his voice.

"You like that?"

"You know I do."

He chuckled again, the low, deep rumbling of it sending another wave of sensation through her to peak her nipples and part her thighs. He left her center long enough to shuck out of his boxer briefs and pull off her panties before he slid back behind her again. Now, with nothing between them, his pulse throbbed through his cock against her back.

He pulled her harder against him as he shifted his body a bit lower, then came up again to slide his erection inside her. He filled her completely, both of their movements stopping at the initial sensation.

"Mmm."

That noise never failed to come out of her when he entered her, that sighing whisper she was unable to control. He responded with his own sound, now as familiar to her as his laughter, and that also never failed to arouse her.

They moved together without effort, without confusion, his finger circling her clit while he thrust smoothly inside her. Josie bent forward, burying her face into the pillow and opening herself to take more of him inside.

He gave another, harder thrust, moving faster. His hand matched the new pace, fingers sliding over and over her slickened clit, pinching and stroking it in time to every thrust. Her breath caught and she almost forgot to let it go, to breathe. She gasped as he filled her.

He murmured her name, which also never failed to send her closer to the edge. He paused in stroking to capture her clit between his thumb and finger. He tweaked the upright bud, moving it back and forth.

Ecstasy rolled through her, wide, rippling waves of it.

Her cunt clenched on his cock. Everything became Jack, the sound of him, the smell, the feeling of him.

"Jack," she whispered.

"I can feel how close you are," he replied, his already deep voice gone subsonic in his arousal. "Go over the edge for me, Josie."

And she did, sliding into climax with an easiness she'd never had with any other lover. She clutched a handful of the bedclothes and bit the pillow while she cried out from the force her orgasm. One heartbeat, then two, and a third passed while her clit pounded.

Jack eased off, cupping his palm against her instead of using the direct stimulation of his fingers. He pumped into her harder, moving her body with the force of his thrusts.

"One...more...time," he said, each word separated by a breath as his voice shook from desire.

The sound of him feeling as good as she was sent another flare of desire coursing through her, and she was already halfway up the hill when he began to rock his palm against her. He knew just how to work her, how to time his thrusts with the pressure of his hand, how to coax another orgasm out of her.

The second one always took less time, like a stove that had been pre-heated, or an engine already idling. She went from post-orgasmic spasms to a new rush of heat between her legs in seconds. Then she was coming again, more briefly but no less intensely than the first time.

They made it together this time, his final thrust coinciding perfectly with her last fluttering spasms. His hand stilled and he held her close, his teeth on her shoulder.

It took her a few minutes to get her breath back, and he slipped out of her while she nestled back against him. His arm went around her. She waited for the tell-tale sound of his breath changing, waited for him to start sliding off into sleep, but he nuzzled her neck again and held her even closer.

"Love you," he murmured into her hair. "You know that, right?"

"Yes." She turned in his arms to face him, nose to nose and lips to lips. She put her hand up to run over the dark stubble of his hair, down over his cheek to run a finger along his full lips. "Love you, too."

A shadow flickered in his chocolate-brown eyes. He crushed her to him, holding her so tight she momentarily couldn't breathe. She usually loved it when he enfolded her that way. No matter what she might worry about the size of her jeans or the width of her hips, in Jack's arms, Josie always felt petite. Now, though, his hug had a hint of desperation to it, and she couldn't understand why.

She put her arms around him, inhaled his scent, and kissed his chest before pushing away gently so she could get some air. He'd closed his eyes, but his brow still had a furrow in it, his lush mouth touched by the hint of a frown.

"Something wrong?"

He shook his head and kissed her forehead without opening his eyes. "No."

The shadow in his look and the fierce hug had made her ask the question, but his answer set mental alarms blaring. Jack wasn't a good liar, at least not to her. They'd known each other too long for that.

Yet, when any other time she'd have pressed the issue, something about the way he was acting stilled her tongue. Instead, she curled into his arms, her own brow furrowed and her own lips curving down. It wasn't until she felt his heartbeat slow under her palm that Josie could finally relax and slip into sleep herself.

THREE

It wasn't all right in the morning. Jack woke earlier than she did, which on most days was fine, as he had to get into the shower earlier to get ready for work. But not on Sundays, the one day they were pretty much guaranteed they could sleep in. On Sundays, it had always been clearly understood that, even if he woke up earlier, he was not...absolutely, positively not, supposed to wake her up unless the house had caught on fire.

Something was burning, all right, but it wasn't the house. Josie woke to find his mouth on her breast, tongue busy suckling at the nipple. She swam up from unconsciousness, but just barely.

"Gobacktosleep," she tried to mutter, but the words came out garbled and slurred. Her hand found the top of his head, and he seemed to take that as some sort of invitation because he left her nipple and swooped up to capture her mouth.

That woke her up. Josie opened her eyes and her mouth to protest, but couldn't speak around his tongue. The intimacy they shared had always been based on their

long history. She'd seen Jack in more compromising posi-
tions than any woman had the right to have seen her
future husband in. There really was nothing between
them that could ever be embarrassing again. All the
same—

"Morning breath, Jack!" she muttered, moving away
from his kiss. "Come on, what's gotten into you?"

"I want to get into you."

Another time she'd have laughed at his comment, but he
didn't sound like he was being blithe. He kissed her again,
fiercely.

She put her hand on his chest to hold him off her for a
minute, meaning to scold, but the look in his eyes stopped
her. He took advantage of her hesitation to kiss her again,
and she let him, despite the morning breath. Jack was a
phenomenal kisser really, and Josie couldn't resist him. His
lips nibbled hers, his tongue swept inside her mouth. His
large hands came up to cup her breasts.

He nestled himself between her legs and slid inside her
before she even had the chance to protest. By that time,
there was no question she was awake and more than a little
annoyed, but damn it, also aroused. He could do that to her
with the simplest of touches.

"Jack." She'd meant to scold, but his name came out in a
breathy sort of whisper, cut off by his next kiss.

He rolled over, arms beneath her to support her, and she
ended up on top. He thrust inside her, then pushed her
back gently until she sat up with him still firmly seated
inside her.

"I want to look at you. You're so beautiful."

She'd be a real bitch if she complained about him now,
when he was being so sweet...and oh, with what he was
doing with his thumb. Yum. Josie moved with him, her clit

rubbing on his thumb with every thrust. Sweet tension coiled in her loins as Jack urged her toward orgasm.

He took his hand away to hold onto both her hips, keeping her steady while his thrusts got harder. "Touch yourself."

She smiled as she slid her hand down between them to comply. "You love that, don't you?"

"I love you," Jack answered with another slow thrust. "I love to watch your face when you come."

It had taken Josie a bit of time to get used to Jack's penchant for talking dirty, but now she couldn't imagine making love without conversation. Past lovers had been content with or even insistent on silence while fucking; not Jack. The more she said, the more turned on he got. It was just one of the many surprises she'd discovered when turning friendship into love. He'd led her down quite a few new paths in that regard.

"I love when you watch me," is what she said in reply, and bit her lower lip because she knew he thought that was sexy.

Her fingertip found her clit and she rubbed it. She made a noise that Jack echoed, which made Josie smile. Sex noises always did. But her smile became parted lips when she gasped as his movements got faster and harder.

"I love it when you're on top." Jack's hands slid up to toy with her nipples.

She'd closed her eyes to concentrate on the orgasm rushing toward her, but now she cracked one open to peek at him. "You do?"

He made a noise low in his throat. "Hell, yes."

Her hesitation broke their rhythm for a moment, but Jack picked it up again with ease. "I don't have to worry about hurting you."

That sweet sentiment moved her to bend and kiss him. "You don't hurt me, Jack."

His arms came around her, clutching her so hard he almost did hurt her. He stopped moving inside her. "I don't want to ever hurt you, Josie."

Again, unease slithered through her. This was not like Jack, this ooey-gooey sentimentality. She had no time to dwell on it, though, because he started moving inside her again and, in this position, every time he slid in or out, her clit brushed tantalizingly against his taut, ridged stomach.

"Jack..." Her voice was just a shuddery, quavery whisper. Sparkles of pleasure built inside her, turning her to fire, making her entire body shiver with desire.

"Come with me, Josie. I want to feel you come with me."

She did. Her orgasm washed over her like dawn creeping over a mountain, filling every nook and cranny on the face of her and chasing away all the shadows. She kissed him and he kissed her back, both of them gasping inside each others' mouths, stealing each others' breath and returning it with their own.

Silence, broken only by their breathing, surrounded them. Josie snuggled into Jack's neck. His hands moved from her hips to cup her butt, and he rubbed her skin lightly, almost tickling. She sighed and wriggled, not willing to let the moment go, but a few seconds later she knew she'd have to. There were just some facts about making love that couldn't be ignored. Like the fact if she didn't get off him immediately, she was going to have to deal with a sticky mess.

"Gonna take a shower," she murmured, "while you make me breakfast."

"Me, make breakfast?" Jack grinned and ran his hand over her cheek. "You sure you want that?"

"You woke me up way too early. You owe me eggs, at least. And coffee." She smiled back and kissed his fingers before getting out of bed to make the dash to the bathroom. "Toast. Not burned, please."

He rolled his eyes. "You have so little faith in me."

Something made her say, "I have all my faith in you."

His grin, the one that could have made a nun open up her knees, faltered. "I won't burn the toast."

She opened her mouth to say something, but the phone cut her off. Its shrill ring made her wince as she looked at the bedside clock. "It's your mother."

Jack also looked at the time as he hooked his fingers over the phone. "I'm sure you're right."

"Going to shower," Josie said hastily. "Give my love."

Jack rolled his eyes but grinned as he punched the phone's talk button. "Hey, Ma."

It wasn't that she didn't like Jack's mom. Francine Gold was, in fact, like a second mother to Josie. Which was the problem. One mother was plenty. With two of them, both with plenty of opinions on the upcoming wedding and not afraid to share them, Josie's life was rapidly becoming a nightmare. What one mother didn't request, the other one did. And while, so far, the pair of them hadn't argued with each other about any of the plans, they'd both done plenty of arguing with Jack and Josie.

She ran the shower as hot as she could stand it and got in, letting the spray pound away the ache in her neck and back that even glorious morning sex hadn't relaxed. Soaping her net sponge with ginseng-scented shower gel, Josie scrubbed her body, covering all the places Jack had so recently fondled. She washed her hair and used conditioner, rinsed, then added her special once-a-week heated oil. She squirted facial scrub onto her palm and massaged her face, then used a moisturizing cleanser guaranteed to get rid of crow's feet. With the wedding only four months away, she wasn't taking any chances.

By that time, the bathroom had filled with steam so thick she could barely see, but she was pretty sure Jack would have gotten off the phone by now. As she turned off the water and grabbed a towel, however, she heard his voice, still talking. He didn't sound happy.

Avoiding the bedroom seemed the prudent thing to do. Breakfast didn't seem likely just yet either. Josie flossed her teeth, brushed them, rinsed twice. She plucked her eyebrows and smoothed on facial cream. She even took the time to file and trim her nails...all twenty of them.

Jack was still talking. His voice had risen. He sounded mad. Now she paused in the bathroom door, towel tucked around her, trying not to listen, but unable not to overhear.

"No, Ma. Of course not. I'm sorry you think that, but... No. For crying out loud, Ma, no! Selfish? What's so selfish about it? It's my wedding, isn't it? Mine and Josie's. Not yours. And I'd like...Ma, don't. Don't cry, Ma! I'm sorry. Yeah. I'm sorry you're upset, but not about...Ma, if you're just going to keep arguing with me, I'm not going to talk about it with you. Goodbye."

He clicked the talk button and tossed the phone onto the night stand, then rolled back onto his pillow, arms behind his head. He scowled. Josie had never seen him look that way.

"Did you just hang up on your mother?"

He looked up as if just noticing her. "Yeah."

"Jack, why?" Josie came to sit beside him, half in awe

and half in envy. Heaven knew she'd wanted to hang up on Mrs. Gold herself. More than once.

"Wedding stuff. You know how she is. She wants her own way, and nothing else is all right. You know my mother."

Josie also knew Jack, and up until now, the wedding plans hadn't bothered him at all. He was just as happy to have a sit-down dinner as he was to have a buffet meal. A band or a DJ, he didn't care. Bridesmaids' dresses? As long as they wore them, it didn't matter to him what color or what style.

"What did she want that made you so mad?"

He sighed, and Josie was even more startled to see his scowl become a sad frown. He rubbed at his face, then took her hand. He kissed it, holding her fingers to his lips for a long moment before answering. "Just problems with the guest list."

"Again? I thought we went over that with her. And my parents, too."

He shrugged. "Like I said, you know my mom."

"Who does she want to invite this time? The paperboy's second cousin's sister's college roommate?"

Jack laughed, which eased the anxious ache in her stomach. "Something like that, yeah."

"You told her the guest list had been finalized, right? We already ordered the invitations and everything. We barely have room for the people already on the list. We can't add more."

He nodded slowly. "I know. I told her."

"Okay." Josie sighed and flung herself onto the bed beside him. "Can't we just elope?"

He laughed, sounding more like his usual self. "Vegas?"

"Mmm. I was thinking more like the Bahamas. Someplace nice and warm."

"Barefoot on the beach?"

"Ahh. Perfect."

He knuckled her side through the towel's thickness. "No choice of fish or chicken, just a pu-pu platter and a glass of coconut juice."

"I'll pu-pu platter you, you big lunk." Josie pinched his nipple lightly, making him laugh and squirm away from her. "I spent hours...no, days, weeks already, planning this stupid menu. Do you know how many times my mother had to call me back just about whether the garlic dip should be served with pita triangles or toasted wheat crackers?"

"Don't talk about it any more." Jack stretched. "I think I owe you some eggs."

"Oh, hell," Josie said. "Let's just go out for breakfast. Someplace that serves mimosas. I could use a drink."

"Me, too." He kissed her forehead and looked into her eyes. "You know I love you, don't you?"

"Yes." She kissed him back. "And I love you, too."

When he left her to take a shower, Josie lay back on the pillows for a few more minutes before getting dressed. Something was going on with him. She'd never have thought Jack could have the same pre-wedding jitters she did, but it appeared she was wrong. She only hoped that was what was bothering him, and not something else.

FOUR

"But you have to have your cousin Myrna's daughter." Ava Levine crossed her arms over chest and lowered her glasses to look at Josie. "You were Myrna's flower girl."

Josie still had nightmares about it. "Mom, no. I told you already. We're limiting the bridal party. I'm having Mim and Jack's having his best friend Scott. It's simpler that way."

"But..." Ava threw up her hands "Fine. Be that way. Embarrass me in front of the family."

"Mom," Josie said warningly. "You're really starting to tick me off."

Ava looked stunned. "Josephine Minerva, I can't believe you just said that to me. I'm your mother!"

Josie had just about had enough. Between her mom and Mrs. Gold, she was ready to forget the entire wedding altogether. Added to that was the strange way Jack had been acting, and she was tenser than usual.

"And this is my wedding," Josie replied evenly.

Ava gasped. "I just want to be included!"

"Mom, you've been included in every single decision

we've made so far. The problem is not that you want to be included. The problem is you don't just want to offer your opinion. You want to make the decisions! You and Mrs. Gold, both of you, seem to forget Jack and I are adults. And this is *our* day."

Josie didn't think she'd ever seen her mother speechless before, but she was proud of herself for saying what she felt without raising her voice or bursting into stressed tears. It was too good to last. In the next minute, her mother stood and grabbed her sweater from the back of the chair, then snatched up her purse.

"And I can't believe you won't have Myrna's daughter in your wedding when you know how important it is to me!"

Josie tossed up her hands, well aware that was her mother's gesture. "Why? Why on earth is that so important to you? Jack and I are getting married, Mom. Planning our lives! Don't you think there should be something a bit more important about our wedding than whether or not we have a flower girl?"

Josie's mom took a deep breath. "You wouldn't let me invite the Solomans either."

"I don't even know the Solomans." Josie bit her tongue to keep from shouting. "I've never even met them. And to tell you the truth, I don't really care if they invited you to their grandson's bar mitzvah, Mother. They don't know me, and they don't know Jack."

"You and Jacob are practically breaking our hearts with this wedding," said Ava, sounding like she was ready to cry.

Oh, shit. Not only was she being called Josephine, but Jack had been upgraded to Jacob. That was really bad. Josie tried to soften her voice, to soothe her mom. "We're not trying to."

Her mother sniffed. "I don't understand either one of

you. We've given you everything, Francine and I. Honestly, I think she's spoiled him. Maybe that's why—"

"Don't you dare." Josie got up from the table, too. "Don't you dare blame Jack for any of this. If you want to be mad at me, fine. But don't you dare accuse Jack of being spoiled!"

"I think I'd better leave."

"I think you'd better." Josie could tell her mother had expected a different answer, but the truth was, she was as angry as her mom. Probably more. "I'll call you."

"Will you?" Ava paused in Josie's doorway, looking back at her daughter.

"Of course I will."

"And won't you just—" she broke off when she saw Josie's expression. "Fine."

"Fine."

"You're too stubborn," said her mom.

Josie raised an eyebrow. "Wonder who I got that from?"

That, at least, cracked a smile from her mom. "Your father."

"I'll call you," Josie said again, and closed the door behind her mother. Then she went and took a long, hot bath.

FIVE

Josie was still in the tub when Jack got home three hours later. She'd refilled the tub twice in that time, depleting their supply of hot water but not caring. Soaking in the tub with a warm washcloth on her face and the scent of lavender and peppermint mingling, the bathwater slick with oil, she tried, without success, to relax. The tub was one of the best things about their apartment. An old, cast-iron claw foot, it was big enough to hold two and kept the water hot longer than newer tubs did. Filled to the rim of the overflow spout, it was deep enough Josie could submerge to her chin and float. It was the only thing she'd miss when they moved from their apartment.

If they moved, she reminded herself as Jack came into the bathroom, stripping off his tie and unbuttoning his shirt. So far, they hadn't even begun looking at houses. He tossed the shirt toward the hamper, but it missed. Leaving it on the floor and hanging his tie on the back of the chair, he knelt next to the tub to kiss her.

"How was your day?" he asked.

"It was so not worth taking a personal day to stay

home." Josie sank down more into the hot water. "I thought I'd work from here, but my mom's visit totally blew that."

"That bad?" Jack made a sympathetic noise and dipped his hand into the water rub her stomach. "What was it about this time?"

"What wasn't it about?" Josie closed her eyes, relaxing under his skilled touch. "I've been living on my own for years now. I mean, holy hell, I plan events for a living, Jack. I think I can manage to plan this wedding."

"They need to know ahead of time so they can analyze it five hundred ways. Preachin' to the choir, babe. I know."

And it's worse for him, she thought. With no brothers or sisters to diffuse the situation, Jack got all of his mother's attention. Josie sighed. Jack grinned.

"I've been in the tub since one o'clock," she confided.

He lifted her hand. "Wrinkled fingers." He kissed each one, drawing the forefinger between his lips to suck it gently. "Nice and clean."

"I thought you liked it better when I was dirty," Josie breathed, his mouth sending instant arousal flooding through her.

"Just one more thing I love about you," Jack said, doing the same nibble-suck to her next finger. "How well you know me."

"The water's still warm. Want to join me?"

He took off his pants and got in. The water level rose to the tub's rim, then sloshed over. Josie rolled her eyes.

"You'll clean that up, I presume?"

"Your wish is my command." Jack slid down along the tub's opposite side, his long legs sticking up. "Come here."

She turned to float toward him. More water splashed out. He gathered her against his chest, tucking her head against his shoulder. It wasn't comfortable, really, but worth the cramped knees to be so close to him.

His hands smoothed over her oil-slick skin. The double-thump of his heartbeat pulsed under her palm, and in seconds, it seemed as though her own pulse timed itself to his. Breath in, breath out. Thump-thump. Like clockwork dancers, always moving in time.

"You're not going to change your mind, are you?"

A flippant reply rose to her lips, but stilled when she heard the real concern in his voice. "Of course not. Why would I do that?"

His broad shoulders shrugged, moving her with them. Water splashed. "Sometimes I worry you're going to leave me, that's all."

That made her sit up so fast she slid. "Why, Jack?"

His dark eyes looked guarded. When had she ever looked into them and not been able to know his thoughts? But now she couldn't glimpse them, and it scared her.

"I've known you since we were kids," she said. "There isn't anything about you that I don't already know. I've seen you at your worst and your best, Jack. I love you. What on earth could possibly change that now?"

He closed his eyes, leaning back against the tub's rim. "You never know when things could change. I could do something awful. You could find someone else."

The water had cooled, but that wasn't why Josie's skin went cold. "Are you planning on doing something awful? Do you think I'm looking for someone else?"

"No!" His eyes flew open, and he gripped her tightly. "No, Josie."

"Then why say it?" Tears thickened her voice. "Are you having second thoughts?"

"No." He shook his head slowly, then grimaced. "Of course not."

She put her hand to his cheek. "I love you, Jacob David Gold. I've loved you since we were eight and you dared me to eat a worm."

That made him smile. "You ate it."

"And you puked, watching." Josie slid closer, moving onto his lap to straddle him, knees pressed against the tub's hard porcelain sides. "And when we were ten and you fell out of the tree in Mrs. Dunwoody's yard, who ran for help?"

"You."

"And when we were thirteen, who beat up Sheldon Spankowicz for snapping my bra straps and calling me Plumpy?"

"Me."

"Jack, we've been there for each other forever. What makes you think any of that could change?"

He sighed, his eyes shuttering against her again. "I don't know. Nothing, I guess."

His grin was at half-wattage, and while it was a smile that could still make ladies swoon, it didn't fool her. She kissed him, teasing his full lips open with nibbles and the tip of her tongue.

"I have not suffered eight months of wedding planning hell for anything to go wrong now."

He opened his mouth under hers, his tongue dipping between her lips to stroke hers. "Ah. Right."

He hardened against her, and she rubbed herself along his cock. "You're stuck with me, Jack. Like apples and honey, like chicken and soup, like bagels and lox."

"Like matzo and balls?"

She wrinkled her nose, but kissed him again anyway. "Like that, yeah."

His arms came around her. "I love you."

"I love you, too."

Forehead to forehead, they stared at each other for a long moment. He brushed her lips gently with his. His fingertips traced light circles on her skin, making her nipples perk.

"Josie?" he murmured.

"Mmmhmm?"

"My balls are shriveling in this freezing water. Let's get out."

She laughed. "Heavens, we don't want your balls to shrivel. You might need them."

"Yeah?" He nipped her chin before kissing her lips again.

"Oh, yes. For the sex."

"Yeah? The sex?"

"The multiple orgasm part especially."

"You're going to give me multiple orgasms?"

She nodded, putting on a serious face. "I was thinking of myself, but sure."

"Selfish minx."

"Not selfish. Just...expectant."

Josie got out of the tub and handed him a towel. Watching him get out of the water, she couldn't help the thrill seeing his naked body always gave her. Jack was perfect in every line. Broad shoulders, muscled arms and chest, tight eight-pack abs. An ass just made for grabbing, strong thighs, long legs. Nice toes. He grinned and slid his tongue along his lips in the gesture that never failed to make liquid heat puddle in her pussy.

"Last one to the bed goes down on the other."

"Hey!"

But he was already off, barreling through the doorway,

leaping over the cat and landing on their bed. He grinned as he lay back against the pillows, stroking his erection lightly, waiting for her. Josie took her time, ambling over to the bed and staring down at his body with one eyebrow raised.

"Very nice, Agent Gold," she said in a British accent. "But I fear I must insist upon further negotiations to our contract."

He played along. The game was one they'd played for years, begun one day on a long bus ride home from college. Since becoming lovers, they'd incorporated it into their lovemaking.

"Gold does not negotiate with criminals." He stroked his cock more firmly. "You should know that by now, Agent Levine."

Josie licked her lips and let her gaze travel the entire length of his body before responding. "I was granted a full pardon, Agent Gold, as you well know. I'm no more a criminal than you are."

He paused in his stroking. "A criminal is merely a spy who works for the wrong side, Agent Levine."

Josie reached into her nightstand drawer and pulled out a long crimson scarf, then a black one, both silk. "But who's to say which side is the wrong one?"

She almost cracked up, but kept on her agent face. This game was fun, more so because Jack was a complete James Bond maniac and could not only do the accent of a British spy, but the attitude as well. Even bare-ass naked. She, on the other hand, couldn't manage to keep a straight face, even when Agent Gold wasn't trying to torture information out of her using his classified sexual techniques. The game also became a challenge to see who'd break character first. She usually lost.

"What's that?" Jack asked, hitching higher on the bed.

"Something to keep you still...while I get the information I need."

He laughed, low and throaty, and, damn him, still in character. "Try as you might, Agent Levine, you won't get me to talk."

"No?" She raised a brow at him, trying for Lara Croft instead of Mary Poppins and finding herself sort of in the middle. "We'll just see then, shall we?"

He didn't protest when she tied his hands to the headboard with the red scarf and used the black one to cover his eyes. She'd never done that before. His cock, if anything, got even harder. Her nipples were like iron spikes, her pussy slick with arousal.

"Now, Agent Gold, I demand to know where you've hidden the information."

"You'll have to try harder than that, Agent—" His words cut off into a gurgle as she took his entire length down her throat.

Josie let his cock slide out of her mouth almost the whole way, sucking gently on the tip before sliding her lips all the way down to his balls again. His dark pubic hair brushed her nose and she inhaled the scent of him, bath oil and that musky, perfect smell that was simply Jack. She stroked his sac all along the seam and his hips lifted.

"I still won't tell you." His voice was strangled, the accent slipping just a bit.

She grinned around his dick and sucked it again, letting her teeth scrape a little along the thin skin. He groaned. She looked up at him, the black cloth obscuring his eyes.

"Talk," she demanded. "Or the results won't be pretty!"

For one moment she thought she might actually have made him forget to play the game because she stroked his cock in one firm fist as she spoke and he hissed, arching into her touch. But the next minute he'd recovered. He was too damn good.

"I'll never reveal the location of the Tit Top Diamond!"

That made her laugh. She'd never heard of the Tit Top Diamond. Jack was quick. She thought fast. Winning wasn't everything—it had been quite some time since they'd won points for predicting how they'd get hit on in bars. But winning was awfully fun, and Josie intended to take every advantage she could.

"Talk!" she ordered before she went back down, opening her throat to take his entire length. Down to the base, then up, adding an extra bit of suction at the tip, using her teeth, following every suck with a stroke of her hand.

His cock got even harder under her tongue and lips. She paused to breathe, using both hands to stroke downward, one after the other, so that it felt, for him, as though he were constantly entering her.

"Where is the diamond?" she demanded, forcing her voice to be stern, though it still came out throaty. She was so wet for him. Sucking him off always turned her on because he was so appreciative of it. Hearing the noises he made and watching his face could almost make her come from that alone.

"...never...tell..."

Ooh, he was good. She bent back to take him in her mouth, her fingers stroking the base of his balls again. Her fingers drifted a bit further back, and she was struck with a sudden inspiration.

"I think I know where you've put it," she said between licks and nibbles on his prick. Her fingers circled gently on his perineum. She grinned, knowing he couldn't see her.

"I won't—"

His words became a gasp that ended in a strangled cry

as she slid her mouth along his erection, working her tongue against it and sucking. At the same time, she pressed her finger against his anus, not entering him, just creating a firm pressure that rocked in time to her mouth's movements.

"Josie!"

She'd won, but Josie didn't take the time to congratulate herself. His cock had swelled in her mouth and she worked it faster, suckling, licking, nibbling and stroking as she continued to press her finger against him in the rhythm that matched his thrusting hips.

Jack muttered a string of curses, the words tumbling out garbled and jumbled, and interspersed with hissing breaths. She kept the pace steady, following the clues his body gave her. The curling toes, the bucking hips, the beat of his pulse. He was going to come. She knew his body's responses as well as she knew her own. The way he'd responded to her pressing finger surprised and pleased her that she could so surprise and please him.

His cock swelled just one bit more and he came. Her named echoed in the room as she took all of him, loving him with her mouth and hand until he'd spent himself and twitched beneath her.

She gave him one last, gentle lick and withdrew, moving up the bed to pull off the blindfold and the scarves. He blinked and fell onto the pillows, still breathing hard.

"Damn," he said after a minute. "You got me."

Josie giggled. "The steadfast Agent Gold succumbed to Agent Levine's torture, huh?"

"Hey, I still didn't tell you where to find the Tit Top Diamond."

She tapped his chest. "I found it anyway, didn't I? Who'd have thunk a special agent would put it up his—"

"Damn, Josie!" Jack stopped her with a kiss. "You got me, yes. Okay? Satisfied?"

"Are you satisfied?" she teased.

"Hell, yeah." He grinned and leaned back. "I'm not going to ask where you learned that."

"I told you, those magazines in the doctor's office," she replied without hesitation.

Jack sighed, one hand flung up over his eyes. "Damn, damn, damn."

That made her laugh.

He peered at her. "Don't laugh. You're going to get yours in about two minutes."

"Ooh, I hope so. Not sure I can wait two minutes—"

He growled and rolled over on top of her, pinning her arms above her head. His kiss left her unable to speak, and when he pulled away, his smile made her grin in return.

"You going to tie me up?"

"No. I want you wiggling."

She smiled. "I'll do my best."

He kissed her mouth, then trailed his lips down her chin, her neck, over the slopes of her breasts. He paused to suckle each ripe nipple until she writhed, then left the tight nubs to slide his tongue down her stomach. Sometimes he liked to tease her, kiss her everyplace but on her clit, but he didn't do that today. He centered his mouth directly on the tight flesh, kissing then licking it in the smooth, regular strokes he knew she loved.

Josie parted her legs and lifted herself to his mouth. Jack's hands gripped her hips, controlling her movements to coincide with his magic mouth. He alternated between flat, smooth strokes and quick, flicking licks, until she was shuddering on the edge of orgasm.

Then he eased off, breathing on her. He slid a finger

inside, then another, and bent back to suck gently on her clit while he stroked her inside. Electric pulses of climax crackled through her. She felt like she could have lit up the room like lightning. She said his name, found the top of his head with her hands, urged him to finish her.

He did, sending her over the edge with one last tweak on her clit. He kept his mouth pressed to her, but didn't move it, letting her orgasm fill her without trying to further stimulate her. He knew just how to touch her and when to stop, how much to give without making it uncomfortable. It was skill and experience, but more importantly, it was love.

Jack loved and wanted to please her, so he learned how. The same as she did for him. As her body's tension released, she relaxed, surprised tears leaking from her eyes.

She wiped her face, not wanting him to think she was crying. The love of her life noticed anyway, and cradled her in his arms immediately.

"What's wrong, Josie?"

"Nothing." She couldn't quite explain that her tears came from a joy so deep and profound it made her want to cry. That didn't make sense. "Just loving you, that's all."

"Loving you, too," Jack answered, and pulled the covers up over both of them.

Cocooned in the warmth, snuggled against his heat, Josie slept.

SIX

Rabbi Zendel shuffled through the paperwork on his desk, then looked over his half-glasses at Jack and Josie. "I'll need both of your Hebrew names for the ketubah, the marriage contract. And Jacob, I'll need your conversion certificate. You have one, right?"

Jack nodded. "I'll get it from my parents."

The rabbi gave him a look. "You do realize that if you don't have one, I won't be able to perform the ceremony."

Josie frowned and put her hand over Jack's. "Rabbi Zendel, I'm sure the Golds have all of Jack's paperwork."

Not that he should need it, she thought with a scowl. Jack had been raised Jewish since his adoption by the Golds when he was an infant. Sure, neither she nor Jack were particularly religious, but they were having a religious ceremony, weren't they? Making the effort?

"I need it by the end of the week."

"I'll get it to you," Jack said, unperturbed. His fingers twined with Josie's, keeping her still. "Not a problem."

The rabbi looked at both of them, then back at his

papers. He shuffled them for a bit, then looked back at them again. "Is there anything else you want to ask me?"

Josie looked at Jack, surprised by Zendel's brusque attitude. "I don't think so."

"Okay, then, I'll see you two in a couple weeks to go over the ceremony. You'll be having the bedeken de kallah? The veiling of the bride?"

"Sure, yes." Jack shrugged, looking at her. "If Josie wants it."

"It's part of the ceremony."

"Then we'll have it." Josie got up to shake his hand. The rabbi didn't stand, just shook her hand half-heartedly and went back to looking at his papers.

Josie tried not to let the rabbi's attitude bother her, but Jack must have sensed some of her agitation because, when they got home, he bustled her into the bedroom and lit a few candles in her favorite scent, then handed her the remote control and tucked the covers under her. In a few minutes he was back with a tray holding a mug of hot tea and some chocolate cookies. He settled it on to her lap.

"Cookies? Do you want me to not fit into my dress?" But she ate one anyway, relishing the sweetness mixed with the tea's strong flavor.

"Fuck the dress." Jack stretched out beside her. "Fuck the wedding. Fuck the reception. Let's run away to the Bahamas, like you said."

His head rested on her shoulder, so she couldn't see his face. Josie stroked his head. "We can't."

"I know."

"Believe me," she whispered, her lips against his head, "if I thought we could get away with it without a million years of guilt, I would."

"I know." He snuggled closer, rocking the tray.

The tea spilled, but it was no longer hot so it didn't burn. She wiped at the spot on the comforter with her napkin. Josie stroked his head, feeling the scruff under her palm. He needed to shave again.

"Will you call your mom for the papers the rabbi needed?"

She felt him tense briefly.

"Yeah. I'll get them."

"Want me to call?"

He looked up at her and grinned. "Now, that's how you know it's true love. When someone offers to face your dragon lady of a mother."

"She's not the dragon lady." Josie laughed. "I believe that title goes to my mother."

"Nah. Gorgon. That's your mom."

Together they laughed, and she was reminded once again of how much she really did love this man. No wedding hassles or arguments over catering or bridesmaids could change that. She put the tray aside and slid down in the bed to kiss him soundly on the mouth.

"What's that for?" he asked, expression pleased.

"For being my best friend."

Jack pursed the mouth that had made so many ladies swoon, but now belonged to her alone. "That's it?"

"And my lover." She knuckled his side. "And my future husband."

Jack pretended to shiver, but drew his finger down her cheek. "That sounds awfully serious."

"It is."

He rubbed his thumb against her lips until she bit at it playfully. "Maybe we should serve worms at the reception."

He cut off her laughter with a kiss that turned hot, fast. He pulled her on top of him, his large hands cupping her ass and pressing her into his erection. She wriggled on top of him until he held her still, growling and nibbling. He positioned her so his dick thrust upward between them and rubbed against her clitoris. Her slickness coated both of them, making it easier for him to slide her along his length, back and forth.

After a bit she lifted herself as he thrust upward, and when she came down she slid with ease onto his cock. As always, it fit her just right. "Like Goldilocks," she murmured, a little hazed from arousal.

That made him laugh. "What?"

She laughed, too. "Goldilocks...this one is just right."

"You're comparing my cock to a bowl of porridge?"

She moved on him, putting her hands on his chest to support herself while she did. "It's hot, isn't it?"

He pumped inside her. "But it's not soft."

"Tastes sweet," she whispered, bringing her mouth down to his ear. Bent forward like this, her clit rubbed tantalizingly on his stomach.

His hands gripped her hips, but he let her set the pace. She took it slowly, wanting it to last, teasing herself. She put her hands on his shoulders, her hair falling down around her face to tickle his. One hand left his hips to push the long strands over her shoulder, and his hand followed it, sliding down her arm and then her side, back to her hip.

His touch left electric tingles in its wake. Her nipples tightened further. Her clit swelled as she rubbed it against him. His cock stretched her.

"You're so wet," Jack murmured. "I love feeling how wet you get when I make love to you."

She couldn't answer. It was another game she usually lost—Jack could speak right up until the end, but Josie often lost her voice when swept away by pleasure. She moaned, instead, which made him smile.

He tightened his hands on her hips as her pace quickened. "I love hearing that noise."

She did it again, partly to please him and partly because she couldn't help it. His chuckle made her smile in return, but she didn't speak. She didn't have to. Jack knew just what to do for her.

Her focus narrowed, narrowed, to the spot between her legs. She sat back, her clit so engorged she no longer needed direct stimulation on it. The pressure of his cock inside her was enough to spiral her closer to the edge.

She looked down at him and lost herself in his dark eyes. It seemed like she'd been looking into Jack's eyes for as long as she could remember. There was no emotion she hadn't seen in his gaze: anger, sorrow...but best of all, love.

"Love you," she gasped out, rocking with him as he thrust harder.

"Love you, too." He shuddered and pulsed inside her.

Her entire world shrank to that one small spot between her legs. She cried out, fingernails digging into his shoulders. Her cunt spasmed, clenching his cock, and he said her name in a breathy half-gasp that sent another bolt of pure pleasure through her.

A moment later he gave a final thrust, signaling his release. She bent forward to kiss him, and another climax rippled through her, smaller and more diffuse but no less fantastic than the first.

"Again?" he whispered, and she laughed breathlessly into his ear.

"Yes. It's not a contest, Jack."

"Point of pride," he answered. "If I could make you come ten times every time we made love, I would."

"Only ten?" She laughed again and slid off him, mindful of how she positioned herself to prevent a wet spot on the sheets. She usually got up and went to the bathroom right away, but she was feeling so boneless she couldn't quite convince herself to move.

"I'm not a machine, Josie."

She ran her hand down his chest. "Yes, you are. You're the Jackhammer, remember?"

He grimaced, this time at her mention of a past joke. "Don't start."

She giggled. "Isn't that what she called you?"

"She" was Jack's college girlfriend, Sheila Goode. Though she and Jack had only dated for a few months, the stories their relationship produced had become part of the Gold/Levine Canon. The stuff of legend almost. Sheila had been sexually insatiable, a Goth girl with multiple piercings and a penchant for wearing black.

"Don't ask like you don't know."

Josie giggled again. "I bet you wouldn't wear black eyeliner and fishnet shirts if I asked you to."

"Shut up!"

She tickled him until he squirmed. "Too bad. I thought you looked hot."

He flipped on his side to look at her. "Get the fuck out."

She laughed harder at his use of shocked profanity. "Oh, yeah. All moody and stuff. All angsty and Robert Smith from The Cure. Back when you had hair."

He rolled his eyes. "That girl used me up and wore me out. That was probably the worst six months of my life."

She mimicked his expression. "Oh, yeah. Being fucked to death is every man's nightmare."

He frowned. "It wasn't the fucking. It was the hot wax and razor blades. That girl was crazy."

She raised an eyebrow. "I knew about the hot wax. You never told me about the razor blades."

He slanted her a familiar grin. "You never asked."

"That's...kinky."

"That's just scary." He pulled her closer. "Anyway, I was only with her because you were going out with what's-his-name."

"Stuart." Josie snuggled closer. "Don't ask like you don't know."

He laughed, rubbing her shoulder. "We wasted too much time."

"Nah." She grinned up at him. "We would never have made it in college. Then what would've happened?"

"You don't think so?"

He sounded so genuinely curious she pulled away to look up at him. She'd thought it had always been mutually understood that their relationship had grown from friendship to love through the years. She'd never guessed he might really have thought differently in college.

"I think so," she replied matter-of-factly.

"Why not?"

"Because you were interested in partying and drinking and hooking up," she told him. "And I was trying to figure out exactly what I wanted to be when I grew up."

She'd changed majors three times in college. Jack, who'd excelled scholastically despite his social proclivities, had never wavered from the major he'd decided on his junior year of high school.

It was the way he'd always been, though. He set his sights on a goal and he reached it, no matter how long the road to get there or how many times he stopped along the side of it. Her path had been different, a winding garden lane instead of a mega-superhighway. Yet they'd both ended up in the same place.

She kissed his warm, bare shoulder. "We are the sum of our experiences. If we hadn't lived our past, we wouldn't be here now."

"Tell me you couldn't have done without Stuart."

She laughed lightly, smoothing his chest under her fingertips. "But then I'd never have figured out I didn't want to pursue medicine. I'd never have taken that course in catering management. I wouldn't have the job I have today, and I love my job."

"And if I hadn't been Sheila's Jackhammer?"

That one was harder. "Um....you wouldn't have learned you're not into kinky sex?"

He gave a mock growl and rolled over on top of her, holding her arms above her head. "Who says I'm not into kinky sex?"

She giggled. "Okay. How about this? You wouldn't have started working out so much. You needed your strength to keep up with her, remember? If you hadn't been with her, you'd still be a skinny, flabby mess."

"With a tremendous 'fro," Jack added.

"That, too. So you see? Thanks to her you became the buff, bald god I see before me."

He laughed and kissed her thoroughly. "So the truth comes out. You only love me because of my body."

"I love you because of your body," she agreed. "And your mind. And your heart."

He smiled. "But the body helps, right?" He let go of her arms to sit up and flex his muscles. "Makes you horny, right?"

She made a face. "Oh, yes."

Jack lay down next to her and pulled the blankets up

over them both. He turned on his side and pulled her close to him, his face serious.

"You're the only person who knows all of me, Josie."

His quiet words made her smile, and she touched his mouth with her fingertips. "Same here."

He pulled her close, tucking her head beneath his chin. "I still don't think you needed to go out with Stuart."

She laughed, snuggling closer, her eyes already drooping. "Go to sleep, Jackhammer."

His chuckle was the last thing she heard before she slipped into dreams.

SEVEN

"I brought a few samples for you to look over," said Mrs. Gold from across the table. Her bracelet clinked on her water glass as she reached to hand Josie a folder. "Daddy and I thought we'd go ahead and order the stationary now so you could get a head start on addressing your thank you card envelopes."

Josie caught Jack's glance and almost heard his words in her head. At least she was asking them before she ordered it.

Josie took the folder. She'd always thought Mrs. Gold was pretty mild-mannered, until the wedding plans began. She'd seen her and Jack in their share of arguments, but it wasn't until the past few months she'd appreciated why.

She took a deep breath and put a smile on her face. "Actually, I was just going to pick up some plain cards from the store..." She pulled out the first set of samples. Creamy ivory paper with embossed letters of raised gold. She brushed it with her fingers. "This is really pretty. Oh, but this one wouldn't work."

She held up the card with the ornate 'G' on the front.

"No?" Mrs. Gold frowned and looked over her glasses. "Too fancy?"

"No." Josie chuckled and sifted through the other samples. They were all ornate. "The letter. My last name starts with 'L.'"

"Sure, it does now," put in Mr. Gold. "But after you're married it won't."

Josie shot a look at Jack, who gave the faintest of shoulder shrugs and the minutest of eye rolls. She frowned. He hadn't told them.

"I'm not changing my name," she said, figuring it was best to be upfront.

You'd have thought she'd said she was going to sacrifice a virgin by the expression on their faces. She bit her lip against a smile. It wasn't funny, nor was it unexpected. It was just...melodramatic.

"Not? Why? What, what, what?" Mrs. Gold's voice made the diners at the other tables turn to stare.

"Ma," Jack said impatiently. "Calm down."

"What, you don't like the name Gold?" Mr. Gold's tone was blustering and teasing, but Josie knew he was serious.

"I love the name Gold," she said soothingly. "But my name is Levine. It's the name I've had all my life. I like it."

"It's a fine name," said Mrs. Gold in a wavering voice. "But you're getting married, Josephine."

Oh, shit, there it went with the Josephine thing again. "Francine," she said gently, "lots of women keep their names after they get married."

"Jack?" Mrs. Gold asked.

At least they hadn't graduated to Jacob, which showed her they weren't blaming him for her waywardness. At least, not yet.

"Josie is allowed to call herself by any name she wants,"

Jack said firmly. His hand found hers under the table and squeezed. "It's her name."

"But what about the children?" Mrs. Gold cried.

"They'll have Jack's name," Josie replied quickly. Not that they were thinking of kids any time soon. "No worries."

Mrs. Gold's fingers plucked at her napkin. "Well, then I suppose I'll have to use that stationary for myself."

"Ma!" Jack cried. "Why'd you order it without talking to us first?"

Her mouth thinned as she glared at him. "How was I supposed to know she wasn't going to change her name?"

"You could've asked," Jack shot back. His hand tightened on Josie's, crushing her fingers together against the metal band of her engagement ring. She winced.

"Jacob," said Mrs. Gold.

And that was it, Josie thought. It took a lot to make Jack mad, but when he got there, it wasn't a pretty sight. She just sat back and kept her mouth shut, sharing a commiserating look with Mr. Gold, who'd certainly suffered through enough of the battles between his son and his wife to know what to expect.

"I only wanted to do something nice for the two of you," Mrs. Gold was saying plaintively.

"No, Ma. You wanted us to send thank you notes on the cards you picked out. You had no intentions of finding out what we wanted to use."

"What, it's so wrong to want to buy you a gift?"

"Then you should've just given us the box, Ma, instead of pretending you cared what we liked."

Mrs. Gold sniffed. "Well, it's a good thing I did ask, isn't it? Since you can't use them anyway?"

"Then don't complain about the fact you bought them," Jack snapped. He let go of Josie's hand and pushed his chair back, lacing his fingers behind his head. "God, Ma, you can be so sneaky sometimes."

Even Josie gasped at that line. She bit down on her exclamation, not because she didn't agree with him, but because saying it sounded so harsh. But it seemed Jack had been pushed to his limit. While Josie and Mr. Gold knew well enough to back away, Mrs. Gold had always seemed a bit blind to her son's hot buttons.

"I can't believe you'd say such a thing to me," she said.

"I can't believe you'd really think I was too dumb to figure out the truth," Jack replied.

Josie and Mr. Gold shared another look. All of this over some stupid stationary? The news she meant to keep her name would have come out sooner or later, but the cards hadn't been that big of a deal. She'd have used them if it meant keeping out of an argument.

"Jack," Mr. Gold placated. "Francine, please. Both of you."

Jack looked around the restaurant as if noticing their raised voices were attracting attention. "Never mind, Ma. Just forget it."

"I will not—" Mrs. Gold began, but Mr. Gold stopped her.

It was the first time Josie had ever seen Jack's father interrupt one of his wife's tirades. Mrs. Gold seemed as surprised as Josie.

"Francine, enough. Let it go."

"Fine," Mrs. Gold said stiffly. "Fine, I'll keep the stationary. You can buy your own, whatever kind you want. Forget I tried to do you a kindness."

Josie had always seen Jack bend at this point, but apparently he hadn't packed his suitcase for this particular guilt trip. He only stared at his mother for a moment so long and silently it made Josie want to say something just to cover up the awkwardness.

"It's not about the cards," he said finally and stood up. He tossed his napkin to his plate, then left the table.

Josie watched him go in stunned amazement, his tall, broad figure easy to follow as he wove his way through the crowded restaurant. She looked back at the Golds. She'd been witness to arguments before, even ones that had gotten more heated. At this point, she expected to see Mrs. Gold in tears. Jack's mother stared at her plate, a stony look on her face.

Whoa. Supremely uncomfortable. Josie cleared her throat, trying to think of something to say.

"You should go after him," said Mr. Gold, surprising her again. He jerked his head in the direction Jack had gone. "Go ahead, Josie. We'll take care of the check."

She didn't argue. "Thanks, Ben."

He smiled. "He's just like his mother."

Mrs. Gold sighed and frowned, not looking at Josie. "No, Ben, he's not. He's just like me."

Jack's adoption had never been a secret, but Josie had never heard Mrs. Gold reference it before. She didn't know what to say. She gathered her coat and her purse and left the restaurant to find Jack.

She found him by the car, smoking a cigarette. That shocked her. Jack had smoked occasionally in college, more socially than anything else. He smoked when he drank. In the past few years, he'd stopped doing even that.

He took one last drag and pitched the butt to the ground, grinding it out with his foot. "Hey."

"Hey." She looked at the crushed cigarette. "Where'd you get that?"

"Bummed it off the waitress on the way out."

She raised her brows but said nothing. Jack put his hands in his pockets. "Are they coming out, too?"

"I don't think so."

He sighed and ran his hand over his head. "Fuck it all, Josie. Why do I let her get to me that way?"

Josie laughed. "Oh, honey, your mom means well."

He shook his head. "She thinks she does."

"She does." Josie took his hand. His mom drove her nuts, too, but Francine's motives were usually good. "She just likes to have her own way. Like my mom. Hell, like me."

"Nah." Jack squeezed her fingers. "You're not like them."

That was reassuring to hear. She stood up on her toes to kiss him. "It's cold out here. Let's go."

He nodded and unlocked the doors. When he started the car, he slipped in a disc of music Josie immediately recognized.

"Billy Idol?"

Jack cranked the volume as Rebel Yell poured from the speakers. "It used to drive my mom crazy when I listened to this."

Josie liked Billy Idol, too, but even if she'd hated the peroxide-blond rocker, she'd have kept quiet. Jack was fighting some sort of personal battle. If listening to Billy Idol helped him get through it, she wasn't going to judge.

Soon he was singing along and adding the sneer. Josie smiled, watching. By the time the song segued into White Wedding, she was singing, too.

They finished the song as they pulled into the driveway in front of their apartment. Jack turned off the car and looked at her. He curled his lip.

"Oy. Fancy me rocking the cradle of your love?"

"Flesh for fantasy," Josie replied with a waggle of her eyebrows. "Don't leave me dancing with myself."

"Never," replied Jack Idol with another sneer. "I fancy shagging the stuffing right out of you."

She laughed, glad he seemed to be in a better mood. "Ah. we'll see, won't we?"

"First one inside gets to pick the position," he said, reaching for the door handle.

He was fast, but Josie, faster. Before he could open the door she'd used the power lock button to lock him in. Then she manually unlocked her door, flung it open and jumped out of the car. Laughing at his shout, she slammed the door and dug in her purse for the keys as she ran for the stairs. They lived on the third floor. She'd never win running in heels, and she paused to shuck the shoes.

Jack was fast. She heard the foyer door clang open and she leaped the stairs two at a time, sliding on the polished concrete in her stockings. Her purse knocked against her back, but she flung herself through the door at the top of the stairs as she heard his feet pounding behind her.

Laughter made her clumsy, and she dropped her keys. Scrambling to pick them up, she dropped her purse. The contents scattered everywhere, lipsticks and change clattering on the polished wooden floor.

Jack banged open the door to the stairs. Josie looked up, keys in hand, and left her purse to defend itself. She slotted the key into the lock, but Jack was too fast. He caught her around the waist and pulled her away from the door, turning her to face him.

"I still won," she managed to say through gasps of laughter that became gasps of another sort when he kissed her.

He shoved her up against the wall next to the door,

pulling his force so he didn't hurt her. He ground himself against her as he slid his mouth down her neck to bite and suck at her throat. His hands went to her hips, pulling her against his erection, and he kissed his way down her body. When he got to her waist he lifted up her skirt and went to his knees, burying his face in her heat so fast and without warning that she yelped.

His tongue found her through the sheer mesh of her panties. His hands clasped the bare skin above the top of her gartered stockings. His thumbs made slow, lazy circles on the inside of her thighs as his lips worked her clit.

She parted her legs for him, back arched against the wall and her hands on his head. The dark stubble of his hair rasped on her palms, one more sensation to enhance her pleasure.

Jack pulled the front of her panties down far enough to reach her bare skin. When his tongue returned to her clitoris, she bent her knees to allow him greater access.

He took it, stroking her with smooth, regular licks that had her quivering. He made a quiet, frustrated noise in the back of his throat and tugged her panties, but couldn't move them beyond the garters. "I hate these things."

"You...bought them..."

He took one side of the sheer panties in his fists. The purring noise as the fabric tore and the subsequent gust of cool air on her skin made the first orgasmic wave ripple through her. "Hey!"

She wasn't complaining. He bent back to her heat, sucking and licking her while he slid a finger inside to press on her g-spot. Just before she started to come he withdrew, knowing how much to give her without sending her over. In the next moment he'd returned to her mouth, forcing her lips open with his tongue and devouring her. His hands fumbled with his belt and pants. He lifted her, back against the wall and skirt hiked to her waist, using his hands to hold her and his cock to anchor her in place.

He stopped when he'd entered her, shifting her weight so she could wrap her legs around him. His hands slid to cup her ass as she curled her arms around his neck. He started moving, each subtle in and out thrust making her back slide against the wall.

"Ahhh, yes." Josie's cry filled the hallway. "Fuck me, Jack."

He did, hard enough to rap her head against the wall. He loved to hear her talk that way. He shoved into her harder, grinding against her. He bit her neck and she cried out, aware he'd actually bitten her instead of merely nibbling, but unable, at that moment, to care.

He immediately soothed the wound with kisses and murmured an apology.

"Shhh," she warned. "Later. Right now, just fuck me harder."

And he did. One orgasm ripped through her, then another right on the heels of the first. Her vision blurred. Jack thrust into her one last time, his entire body tensing and releasing as he came. He held her for a few moments more, then slipped out of her and put her down.

"Wow." Josie pulled her skirt down and pushed the hair out of her eyes. "I'm glad we're the only ones living on this floor."

He laughed and picked up the remains of her panties, and then gathered the contents of her purse, stuffing them haphazardly into the bag. "Sorry about this." He touched the bruise on her throat. "And that."

"Don't be sorry, baby." She took the ruined panties and her purse. "You'll buy me more."

"You could just not wear any," was his suggestion, to which Josie rolled her eyes.

"Right."

Jack used her keys to unlock and open the door to the apartment. "Just saying."

She swatted his ass as he went through the door. "Not gonna happen."

"So soon the magic fades."

She made a rude noise. "Who are you, David Copperfield?"

The blinking red light of the answering machine caught her attention, and she pushed the button. A woman's voice, low and husky came from the machine's tiny speaker.

"Hello? This is Ardelle Hewitt calling for Jack. My number is—"

Jack punched the button on the machine, cutting off the message. "I got that one already."

"Oh?" Josie gave him a puzzled look. "Who was it?"

She had no reason to suspect him of anything but the truth, but when he said, too casually, "A client," her heart stuttered.

"Okay," was all she said, though, because confronting him on the obvious lie would mean learning something she was suddenly certain she didn't want to know. "Um...gonna use the bathroom."

She locked the door behind her. Jack had little concept of bathroom privacy, and if she didn't lock, he'd think nothing of waltzing in on her. She didn't like that when she was using the toilet, and she didn't like it now. She ran some water in the sink—cold—and splashed her face. Tears clogged her throat, but Josie washed them away before they could fall. She splashed again and again until she was sure she wasn't going to cry.

Ardelle Hewitt might very well be a client. They sometimes called him at home, though rarely. She could be a client, like he'd said, but Josie knew Jack too well to ignore the lie she'd heard in his voice. Now the question was not only what he'd lied about, but why?

EIGHT

"Holy crow," said Mim over the phone line. "I know Mrs. Gold can be a little overbearing, but I've never known Jack to talk to her like that."

"Me neither." Josie typed a few more numbers into her invoice, then scowled and deleted them. She tried again, correcting the mistake. "I don't think his dad quite knew what to do."

"Ick." Mim laughed. "Just a few more months, sweetie, and all of this will be over. At least until you have kids."

Mim's laugh made Josie roll her eyes as she struggled with another set of invoices. "Don't you start, too."

"Are we still on for this weekend?" Mim's phone crackled as she hollered something at one of her children. "Sorry. Sammy's getting into trouble."

"Yes. I even made an appointment at one of the shops and told the sales associate what I was looking for. She's going to pull some gowns and set them aside for when we come in."

"Ooh, fancy schmancy. Can't wait. My dear husband's

going to have a great time with the kids." Mim gave an evil laugh. "Or not."

Josie finished settling the plans with her sister and hung up, then concentrated on the rest of her invoices. The to-do list in her planner said she needed to call the caterer, the florist and the photographer, too. The calls were easier than writing the checks after each one. She winced as she subtracted the amounts from her checkbook. Both sets of parents were helping financially, but the bulk of the money was from her and Jack. Even though they'd determined to keep things simple, it all added up.

Her call to Rabbi Zendel wasn't so easy. "I just wanted to make sure you got the paperwork about Jack's adoption and conversion."

She heard the shuffling of papers. "Yes. My secretary left them for me."

"Is there anything else we need then?"

The rabbi sighed heavily. "If you plan on having a custom ketubah I'll need to approve it ahead of time. Otherwise, you can use the one the temple provides."

"That'll be fine." Custom marriage contracts cost hundreds of dollars.

"And you need to let me know if you plan on attending the mikveh before the ceremony."

Josie knew about the ritual bath Orthodox women visited as part of the family purity laws, but she hadn't expected to ever go there herself. "I'm not sure—"

"It might be a nice gesture," said the rabbi peremptorily. "It is a purification ritual. It might be appropriate for you, especially in light of your circumstances."

"My circumstances?" Josie's fingers stilled on her keyboard. "What do you mean?"

"Well, that you and Jack are cohabitating without

benefit of marriage," said the rabbi in a voice oozing with disapproval.

So that was the reason he was so cool. Josie sighed. They'd had the same argument with both sets of parents.

"If you think it would be appropriate, I'll go," she said to placate him. It seemed a simple enough thing to do, and if it got the rabbi off their backs...

"I'll have Mrs. Kohn call you. She's the mikveh attendant."

He didn't sound any more enthused, but Josie tried not to notice. "Thank you, Rabbi."

The mikveh? she thought as she hung up. Visions of long-skirted Orthodox housewives filled her mind. She sighed. Oh, well. It wouldn't kill her to get purified.

NINE

"If you want to," was what Jack said skeptically when she told him what she'd agreed to. "Hope you don't melt."

She swatted him for that not-so-subtle insinuation she needed purifying. "You could go, too. Lots of men do."

He rolled his eyes. "Right. And I'll grow my sideburns and wear a black hat, too."

"Ooh, sexy." Josie grinned and wiggled her feet, propped in his lap. "I could get myself a wig."

He looked at her. "Nah. I like your hair."

She touched it, tied up into a messy pony tail on top of her head. "I like yours, too."

He ran a hand over his close-cropped head and made a face. "My mom's been trying to convince me to let it grow for the wedding."

Josie slid over onto his lap, her knees pressing into the back of the couch. "Don't. I like it the way it is."

"I'm not going to." He linked his hands around her waist. "What time is Mim coming tomorrow?"

"Early. Around nine."

"And what time will you be done?"

It wasn't like him to badger her with questions about her schedule. "Not sure. Why?"

He shrugged, letting his head fall back against the cushions. "No reason."

"If I don't find a dress tomorrow," she said, "I'm going to wear jeans and a T-shirt that says Jack's Bitch on it in rhinestone letters."

He cracked up, as she'd hoped he would. "And what would mine say?"

"Josie's Manservant," she replied without hesitation.

"In rhinestones?"

"No. Gold sparkly thread."

He laughed and cupped her ass. "I like it when you call yourself my bitch. That gets me so hot."

She pretended to be offended, though at this point there was little he could do, say or ask her that would offend her. "We could just get shirts that say master and slave."

"Yeah, but who gets to where the one that says master?"

"Me."

He tickled her. "I don't think so."

She kissed him. "We'll see, won't we?"

"You'll find a dress," Jack said. "Your sister will sniff one out."

Josie laughed. "I'm sure you're right. Mim is the bargain goddess."

He looked at her seriously. "Don't worry so much about it being a bargain, babe. Get something you want."

That touched her, and she stroked his cheek. "Spending oodles of cash on a dress I'll wear one time only is not really my thing. I'll find a dress. Don't worry. But thanks."

"I just want you to have everything you want," he said, and his sentiment made her throat close with emotion.

"I do." Josie kissed him again.

This time, his lips parted to accept her tongue. His hands moved restlessly along her back, then reached up to tug the band out of her hair and send it tumbling around her shoulders.

He fingered a long auburn strand, then rubbed it across his face. "Your hair always smells so good."

She smiled. "Yours, too."

He tickled her again. "Be quiet, slave."

"Make me."

He grabbed her wrists and pinned them together in one large hand, then kissed her again as he pushed her hands down between them, against his crotch. "See what you do to me?"

She let her lips slide across his cheek to his ear. "It's all your fault I'm no longer pure."

He lifted his hips upward. "Might as well make your trip to the mikveh worth it, huh?"

His mouth went to her throat and into the vee of her T-shirt. He continued to hold her wrists between them, pulling her forward with his other hand and rocking her crotch against his knuckles. Her clit swelled at the pressure of her denim jeans rubbing her there, and soon her breath had grown faster.

His next kiss landed on the mound of her breast, above the lace edge of her push-up bra. He nuzzled her shirt out of the way to find her flesh, kissing and caressing while she arched her back to push her breasts closer to his mouth.

The hand against her back moved lower to slide along her ass as he rocked her steadily against her pinned hands. Then he let go of her wrists, pulling her hands up to put them around his neck as he moved her directly on top of the erection straining his loose pajama bottoms. Then he put both hands on her ass and continued kissing her breasts, dipping down to find her nipples through her clothes and tease them with his lips.

"This was my first wet dream," he mumbled against her skin.

She'd let her head loll back as he worked, but that made her sit up straight. "What?"

His low, deep chuckle went right to her clit, which pulsed. Hot liquid slicked her. "Seventh grade. We had Earth Science together."

She gave a breathy cry as he ground her down on him. "Yeah, I remember."

"In my first wet dream, we were in the lab, getting ready to weigh some rocks, or something, and I was sitting on those low black stools. You came over and straddled me, like you're doing now. And I did this."

He tugged her shirt upward, then off over her head. His mouth went to her exposed breasts, wetting the sheer fabric of her bra. Her nipples were tight, hard peaks that ached under his talented tongue. He pinched one between his lips, and she jerked with pleasure.

"And what did I do?" she managed to say.

"Pretty much what you're doing now. You moaned and said my name."

"Jack," she obliged as he unclasped her bra and took her nipples directly between his lips.

"And when you did, it was like someone had shoved a cattle prod down my pants. I'd never felt anything like that. I woke up with my dick busting a hole in my pjs and stuff shooting out of it."

The thought of it made her smile. "That's a pretty sophisticated dream for a seventh grader."

He pulled away from her breasts to smile up at her. "I guess I was mature for my age."

"I guess so." She thought. "My first sex dream was about Johnny Depp."

He rolled his eyes. "That scrawny little punk?"

"It was the scissor-hands." Josie laughed. "I dreamed he cut all my clothes off and then went down on me."

"What?" Jack seemed genuinely shocked. "You're kidding."

"Nope. That was the first time I ever had an orgasm in a dream."

"In a dream," he repeated. "You'd had one before that? How old were you?"

"Oh, sixteen, probably. And yes, of course." She rocked a bit on his lap, pressing her center against him. "It was much easier fending off boys' advances when I knew I could satisfy myself faster and better and more safely on my own."

"And what about now?"

"Now," she said, nipping his lower lip between hers, "I have you."

He tugged the drawstring of her flannel sleep pants, then slipped his fingers inside. "Yes, you do."

He rubbed her, holding her with one hand while the other performed magic. Her head fell back and she gripped his shoulders, moving her hips in time to his movements. In seconds she was on the edge.

Jack stopped long enough to push his pants down to his shins, then helped her with hers before settling her back on his lap. The back of the couch was soft on her knees. His cock filled her, her clit pressed against him, and his hands lifted her ass so he could thrust in and out of her.

He had her shuddering in under a minute, and when he nudged his thumb between them to caress her clit more firmly as she moved on his erection, Josie cried out. She gripped his shoulders and came, then came again a moment later. Two small orgasms that nevertheless left her breath-less and gasping.

Jack finished a moment later, burying himself inside her heat. "I love you, Josie."

"I love you, Jack."

She smiled and cuddled against him for a moment. "I'm going to take a bath and go to sleep early. What about you?"

He rubbed her back with his strong fingers. "I'm going to stay up for awhile. Maybe watch a movie."

"'Kay." She kissed him again, then slid off. "Good night."

Later, in the bath, she thought she heard him talking on the phone, but by the time she came out, she heard only the sound of some shoot-em-up Friday night feature. She fell asleep before he came to bed, and her dreams were restless and filled with images of scissors.

TEN

Josie had found the perfect dress. She couldn't believe her luck, because the gown not only fit her without need for alterations, but it had been discounted to a price that made Mim shriek so loudly everyone in the store turned to look at her.

"It's fate," Mim said as they entered the restaurant. "I mean, the dress is even called the Josephine."

"After Josephine Bonaparte, no doubt, not for Josie Levine." But Josie grinned as the hostess led them to a small table toward the back. "It is funny, though."

"It's gorgeous," Mim assured her.

The dress was of soft, ivory fabric with puffed short sleeves and an Empire waistline accented by a broad satin ribbon. Pearls dotted the neckline and dangled from the overskirt, which pulled up to reveal a panel covered with embroidered red roses with green leaves.

"I'm sure I'll hear about it," Josie said as the waiter took their orders. "It's not traditional enough. It's not all white. It's—"

"It's you, and that's all that matters." Mim drank her iced tea. "Don't show it to them."

"No?"

"No." Mim nodded firmly. "Mom and Mrs. Gold don't need to see your dress. Because you're right. They will pick it apart even if they don't mean to, and I'd hate to see you lose the joy you get from it."

"That's such a nice thing to say. You're the bestest sister ever."

Mim grinned. "I know."

"They're going to want to see it."

"Too bad." Mim rolled her eyes. "They've had their fingers in every other piece of pie. They don't need theirs in this one."

"You sound a little...bitter." Josie laughed.

"Just used to Mom, that's all."

The talk turned from the wedding to other things. The house hunt, Josie's job, the honeymoon plans, Mim's kids. Finally, Mim looked at her watch.

"I should get going."

"Yeah, me, too. It's already close to two."

The sisters got up. Josie's bladder twinged. "I'll meet you at the car."

On the way out of the bathroom, her entire world shattered. She was weaving through the tables to take a more direct way out of the restaurant, when she spotted a familiar figure. Jack sat in a booth tucked way in the back, but he wasn't alone.

The woman sitting across from him looked like she could be any age from late thirties to early forties. Her dark skin had been expertly made up to accentuate large sloe eyes and full, red lips. She'd pulled her black curls up on top of her head in a loose chignon that managed to be casually elegant and sexy all at the same time. Her simple sapphire colored blouse looked to be of silk and showed off her petite, but luxurious, figure.

She held both of Jack's hands in hers, and she was alternately smiling and crying.

At this angle, Josie couldn't see Jack's face, but she could see his fingers interlacing with the mystery woman's. He leaned across the table to speak to her, then handed her a napkin to wipe her cheeks.

Josie stood frozen. She could not believe her eyes. It couldn't be Jack, not her Jack. It had to be someone who looked like him. He would stand and she'd see, and she'd have a good laugh.

But she didn't laugh when the woman got up from the booth and the man with her did too, and there was no mistaking that it was Jack. No confusing the woman for a client, either, unless Jack was in the habit of kissing his clients, which he now did. Josie watched in stunned horror as he hugged the small woman and kissed her cheek.

So it wasn't exactly a passionate embrace, but clearly, this was not a business acquaintance. He knew this woman, was close enough to her to help her shrug into her coat and walk out with her, arm in arm.

Josie thought she might actually fall down right there in the restaurant, but she locked her knees and kept her back straight. She didn't even cry, couldn't, she was too numb. She made it out to the car and slid into the passenger seat.

"Jojo?"

She couldn't even respond to the awful nickname. "Something at the restaurant disagreed with me."

Mim, bless her, got her home in record time. "Will you be okay?"

Josie assured her sister she would, though she was not,

in fact, certain of that. Once inside her apartment, she splashed cold water on her face to stop the sick feeling, then looked around with a determined eye. She went to the computer and pulled up Jack's email, typing in the password she'd never, until now, thought of using. She scanned the messages, skipping the spam and correspondence from people she knew. She didn't recognize the address, hewittflowers57@finders.org. The subject line was a date. Today.

She paused before she clicked on it, but did anyway. A simple, straightforward message, nothing fancy, but one that sent shards of agony right to her heart.

Jack,

Saturday will be fine. I can't wait to see you. I'll be there by 1.

Love,

Ardelle

Ardelle. The woman who'd left the message on the phone. The one Jack had claimed was a client.

Josie got up from the computer and went to Jack's briefcase. Again, she knew his combination, but had never considered using it before now. The numbers on the dial stuck and she muttered a curse, her fingers fumbling. It was difficult to see through her tears.

The plain manila envelope shouldn't have looked so menacing, but the moment she saw it, Josie knew its contents were going to change her life forever.

"Do you want to do this?" she asked herself out loud. She looked around the empty apartment. "This is Jack. You've known him forever. This is Jack, Josie."

The sound of her words didn't soothe her. In fact, they made her feel worse. Talking to herself in an empty room. Nutty.

She touched the envelope, which was lumpy. If she

looked inside, her questions might be answered—or she might only learn she had more to ask.

Jack had never lied to her before, not about anything major. His faultless honesty was one of the qualities she'd appreciated so much in their friendship and valued in their love.

But he'd lied to her now. She had proof. And still, she couldn't bring herself to look inside the envelope. She set it on the coffee table and made herself some strong, hot tea while she waited for him to get home.

The first words out of his mouth said it all.

"Oh, shit." Jack looked first to the envelope, then at Josie sitting on the couch.

She felt strangely calm now. No tears. She was too numb for tears. "Something you want to tell me?"

"What were you looking in my briefcase for?" Jack ran a hand over his head.

"Valid question," Josie replied coolly. She nudged the envelope with her foot. "I'm sure you didn't expect me to find it in there. I saw you at the restaurant today."

His body sagged. "Ah, damn."

Her voice wavered. "I want to know why you lied to me."

"Josie..."

He made as though to move toward her, but she put up her hand to stop him where he stood. "Why, Jack? What the hell were you thinking?"

He sat in the ratty armchair across from her and put his face in his hands before looking up at her with a haunted expression. "I wanted to tell you, so many times."

"So many times? How long has this been going on?" She put her now-cold tea down with a thump. It splashed.

"I met Ardelle three months ago."

"Three...three months?" She tried to breathe and almost couldn't. "You told me she was a client!"

"I know. I should've told you the truth. I just wanted to keep it to myself for a while, until I got used to the idea."

"Get used—" Josie stood, shaking. "What the fuck, Jack? Get used to what? Who the fuck is she, that you wanted to get used to her? If you wanted out of this, all you had to do was say it! Get used to it?"

"No, Josie, no—" He stood and tried to take her in his arms, but she flung away his grip.

"I saw you together, holding hands! I saw you!"

He looked stunned, first at her face, then down at the envelope "You didn't look inside that?"

"No!" she yelled, furious. "I figured I'd trust you to tell me the truth. Instead, you give me some bunch of bullshit excuses..."

"No, wait. Josie, listen." He ran both hands over his head this time. "It's not what you think."

"No? So who the fuck is Ardelle Hewitt, Jack, that she signs her emails 'love' and holds your hands in a restaurant? If she's who'd you'd rather be with than me, at least own up to it!"

"Rather be with...No. Josie, baby, no." Jack shook his head and reached for her hands, capturing them before she could get away. He held her still until she looked at him. "Ardelle is not my lover, Josie."

"No?" she challenged.

"No." Jack shook his head. "She's my mother."

ELEVEN

Josie looked at the photos of a much younger Ardelle holding a wrapped bundle. "How old was she?"

"Fifteen." Jack picked up another photo, this one more recent, of a smiling Ardelle and two young men. "This is her with her two sons, Bryant and Evan."

Josie looked at the photo. "You look like her."

He shrugged, but smiled slightly. "A little."

Josie sighed, her emotions still tangled. "How'd you find out?"

"The papers from my parents had her name on them." Jack frowned. "They always told me they never knew who she was, or how to get in touch with her. They lied, Josie. Ardelle was my dad's secretary's daughter. She got pregnant by one of the lawyers in my dad's office. They fired him, but then adopted me. They've known all along who my real parents were. They just didn't tell me."

She squeezed his hand. "I'm sure they had their reasons."

He nodded. "I know. And I never really pushed, you know? Because it hurt Mom. I had the adoption and conversion papers because the rabbi needed them, and when I saw the information there, I knew I had to find out more."

"And your mom didn't want you to."

"No. Even after I told her I wanted to find Ardelle and give her the chance to meet me..." His voice broke and he put his face in his hands again. His shoulders shook, and Josie put her arms around him. She'd never seen him cry.

He looked up, brown eyes wet. "I just wanted her to know me, Josie. To let her know I turned out all right."

"Sure, baby," Josie said as she rubbed his back. "Of course."

"But Mom gave me a really hard time about it, saying Ardelle had given up all rights to me when I was born and had never made any effort to see me since. Which was true," Jack told her, "but I still had to know for myself."

"I know, honey." Josie hugged him.

"So three months ago, I managed to hunt her down and contact her, and we've been keeping in touch. She's married with kids, but..." He hitched in another sobbing breath that broke Josie's heart, for she'd never seen him like this ever. "But she said she'd always kept track of me. Through high school, college, whatever. She never contacted me because she didn't want to interfere, but she'd kept up. And her husband and sons always knew. I have...I have two brothers, Josie."

She held him tight. "Oh, Jack. I'm sorry I ever doubted you."

He clung to her, his face hot on her neck. "I should've told you the truth right away. I just wanted to be sure I was doing the right thing before I got you involved."

"It's all right." She held him tight, then kissed his cheek. "I understand."

"I love you, Josie. I would never cheat on you."

"I know." And she did, and must have always, or else she'd have opened the envelope before he came home to explain himself to her. "I know, baby."

His hug nearly crushed her, but she didn't mind. All that mattered was she'd learned the truth. The rest of it, they'd deal with later.

TWELVE

"Ani l'Dodi v'Dodi li." Josie smiled as she said the Hebrew words. "I am my beloved's as my beloved is mine."

Jack slipped the plain platinum band on her forefinger. The cantor sang the prayers. The rabbi read the ketubah and pronounced them husband and wife.

And they were married.

Josie felt like her face was going to split from grinning as she took Jack's hand and turned beneath the chuppah, the wedding canopy, to face the crowd.

"Here we go," Jack said and crushed the glass beneath his heel.

"Mazel tov!" The cheers of the congregation rang in Josie's ears as she took Jack's hand and looked at the crowd.

Josie and Jack's parents had joined them on the bimah for the ceremony, but Josie looked out at the sea of faces. Her sister and brothers and their families. Their friends. Ardelle and her husband and sons. Some familiar and some not so, but all with one thing in common. All shone with joy and love.

And when Jack pulled her into his arms for their first kiss as husband and wife, all she could think about was his arms around her, his mouth on hers, and all the joys ahead of them...starting then.

POT OF GOLD AND EMERALD ISLE

HISTORICALLY INACCURATE, UNAPOLOGETICALLY SILLY, FULL OF ROLLICKING GOOD FUN!

I

"Turn this boat around right now!" Eleanor Fitzwilliam stomped her bare foot so hard on the broad boards of the deck she imagined the sound of her toes breaking.

The man towering over her smoothed the mustache and beard surrounding his arrogant smile. "I don't think so, love."

"Don't you call me that." Eleanor lifted her chin and ignored the rather blatant look of appraisal he was giving her.

Fuming, she turned to face the broad expanse of open sea. Tears clogged her throat, but she refused to let them fall. She'd made her plans so carefully, made certain when she got off this boat it would be in a place she wouldn't be easily discovered. She'd spent the last three days in the hold with the sea pitching beneath her, only to crawl out this morning to the nasty surprise of a sea view when she'd expected land. Not only did she have no idea where she was, she had no idea who the man was before her.

Desperation made her bold. "How dare you? Who do you think you are?"

He gave a deep, courtly bow that was perfect in its presentation but a mockery just the same. "Captain Robin Steele."

"Robin Steele?" She looked over his worn finery, the braids in his long, dark golden hair, then cast a look over his shoulder to the tattered black flag flapping on the main mast. "How clever. And if I told you my name was Miss Understood, would you believe me?"

"Is your name Miss Understood, love?"

"No, it's Eleanor Fitzwilliam, and I'm not your love!"

He gave another bow. "At your service, Miss Fitzwilliam."

"You are not at my service!" Eleanor pressed her lips together to keep them from trembling. Her father had always taught her a brave face made a brave heart.

He put a hand to his heart and gave an insincere pout. "Well, Miss Fitzwilliam, you happen to be a stowaway on my ship. Which means I'll call you whatever I like. *Love.*"

"It's not your boat," she told him with a sniff. "It belongs to my fiancé, Mister Winston Dandrew, and he'll be sorely displeased to find it commandeered with me aboard!"

The pirate seemed unimpressed. "Upset he might be about the ship, but I suspect he doesn't even know you're aboard, love. Not unless a man's britches and a coating of dirt are your usual attire, in which case, I fail to see why the man asked for your hand in the first place. Care to tell me what, exactly, you were doing?"

Words failed her. She turned around and swung at him, but his hand grabbed hers and, in the next instant, she found herself wrapped in his arms.

"You don't want to do that," he said with quiet menace.

His surprisingly white, even teeth shone against the tanned skin of his face and dark amber of his beard. "I get a mite testy when I'm slapped in the face."

Eleanor hadn't grown up with five brothers for nothing. Though her body pressed so intimately against the pirate's she could barely struggle, she could move her knee. She brought it up sharply, right between his legs, and dropped him like a stone.

"How about when you're kicked in the nuggets?" she cried and was off.

"I don't like that much either," she heard the pirate gasp out from behind her, but she didn't stop to see what he was doing.

She had no place to go. The boat was small--a schooner really--nothing more than a few sails and cabin atop a hold filled with cargo. Winston used it to travel between the islands on business.

She reached the foredeck and pivoted with a wince as the rough boards scraped at her bare feet. She'd thought disguising herself as a boy would help her get away unnoticed by her father and brothers, but now she regretted not wearing boots. The pirate had hunched over, but as she watched, he stood and shook himself like a dog shaking off water. Then he set his shoulders in clear determination, and strode toward her.

A sailor, only slightly less grimy but rather less fancy than the pirate captain, stepped neatly from behind one of the masts. He grabbed her arm hard enough to hurt, and Eleanor yelped. "Unhand me, you scurvy swabby!"

The man gripping her arm frowned. "I ain't got scurvy."

Now she noticed the ship's crew. Some dangled from the masts like monkeys, while others knotted ropes and swabbed the decks with nasty-looking mops. She shivered.

"You needn't yank her arm from her shoulders." The pirate's grin was pure evil as he looked at Eleanor. "Though I'd like to let you, Ridley, her fiancé might not take kindly to getting back ruined merchandise."

She had no intention of returning to Winston, but the pirate didn't know that. She certainly didn't want to be ruined, in any case. Eleanor stepped away from the sailor, who went back to his business with a shrug.

"So you'll let me go?"

"Eventually." The pirate peered at her closely. "When I've finished my business."

"Your business!" She gasped at the effrontery of it. "This is my fiancé's boat!"

He looked pained. "Ship, if you please, love. A boat is something you row on a pond. The Rainbow is a ship. And a very fine one at that. One of the finest I've ever borrowed."

"Stolen, you mean! Shanghaied!!"

"Is your voice always so...shrill?" He rubbed at his ear.

"My voice," Eleanor said from between gritted teeth, "is not shrill."

He raised his eyebrows. "It could make paint peel. It could--"

"Oh, close your gob," she retorted smartly and crossed her arms over her chest. "I want to know--I demand to know--when you're going to return me to land!"

The pirate shook his head and held out his hands, palms up. "I told you, love. After my business is completed."

He put a hand too casually on the cutlass hanging from his belt. Eleanor swallowed, hard, despite a mouth gone suddenly as dry as sand. She'd been so stunned to come on deck and find the boat--the ship--out to sea instead of docked at the next island, she hadn't had time to be afraid. Now, however, she watched the pirate's dark eyes sweep over her scantily clad body and her heart thudded.

"What is your business?" she asked in a much smaller voice. Pirates were bloodthirsty brigands. Sailors were notoriously rowdy. She could hold her own against men who at least had a modicum of respectability, but against true buccaneers...

"Gold, of course. What other business could I possibly be about?" He grinned at her again, which did not make her feel any safer. He had a dangerous smile, bright and cheery, in a face she'd have guessed better suited to scowling. "I am a pirate."

"Saddest pirate I ever seen," said the sailor from behind her. "No ship of his own, nary a crew..."

"Belay that talk." The pirate gestured so rudely at the sailor Eleanor had to avert her eyes. She knew what a gesture like that meant, of course. But a lady shouldn't be exposed to such a thing. He looked back at her with an almost apologetic look. "Ridley is a scurvy bilge rat, love. Don't listen to a word he says."

"I ain't got scurvy!" Ridley shouted and stalked away.

The pirate shrugged. "Maybe he's not got scurvy, but his temper's pretty fierce."

Eleanor straightened her back, too aware of the way the salt wind was revealing her body. She wished desperately she hadn't dispensed with her chemise before donning her brother Horatio's cast-off clothes. Now a chill swept her spine at the fresh breeze, and her nipples strained the thin linen shirt. She crossed her arms more closely about her, but that did no good, merely pushed her generous bosom up and out.

"I warn you, if you hurt me, my family will hunt you down. You'll never get away with it."

"I don't want to hurt you, love." He sounded sincere. "I may have gone on the account, but I know how to treat a lady.

Eleanor wasn't particularly reassured, but she pretended confidence anyway. "I demand you take me back, now, and return this boat--"

"Ship."

She glared at him, finding it easier to be angry than afraid. "Ship back to port!"

"We'll get to port all right," the pirate said. "But not the one you're wanting."

He turned away from her, then paused, as if he'd thought of something else.

"And another thing." His voice had gone deep again, low and dangerous. He glanced back briefly, his eyes glittering in a way she found terribly disconcerting. "You may ask me for whatever you wish, and if 'tis in my good nature to provide it, I will. But you demand nothing."

Then he left her standing on the deck while the ship continued to crest through the vast ocean waves.

Pot of Gold and Emerald Isle

ALSO BY MEGAN HART

All Fall Down

All the Lies We Tell

All the Secrets We Keep

A Heart Full of Stars

Always You

Broken

Beg For It

By the Sea of Sand

Castle in the Sand

Clearwater

Dirty

Hold Me Close

Hurt the One You Love

Naked

Passion Model

Precious and Fragile Things

Ride with the Devil

Stumble into Love

The Favor

The Resurrected One: First Come the Storms

Womb

Unforgivable

Pleasure and Purpose

No Greater Pleasure

Selfish Is the Heart

Virtue and Vice

ABOUT THE AUTHOR

photo credit: Whitney Hart Photography

I was born and then I lived a while. Then I did some stuff and other things. Now, I mostly write books. Some of them use a lot of bad words, but most of the other words are okay.

If you liked this book, please tell everyone you love to buy it. If you hated it, please tell everyone you hate to buy it.

Find me here!
www.meganhart.com
readinbed@gmail.com

facebook.com/READINBED

twitter.com/Megan_Hart

instagram.com/readinbed

bookbub.com/authors/megan-hart

goodreads.com/Megan_Hart

Made in the USA
Middletown, DE
28 August 2023

37511715R00110